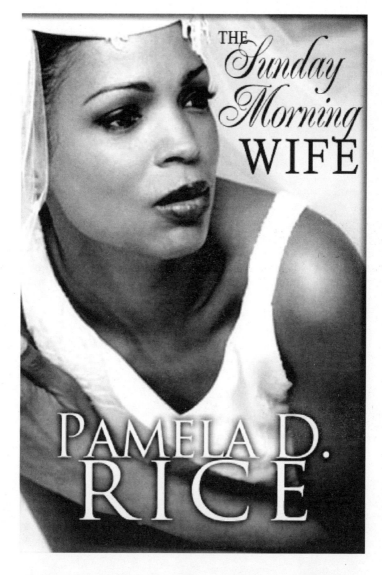

THE SUNDAY MORNING WIFE

A NOVEL BY PAMELA D. RICE

THE SUNDAY MORNING WIFE

A NOVEL BY PAMELA D. RICE

Peace In The Storm Publishing, LLC

Rice

Peace In The Storm Publishing, LLC.
P.O. Box 1152
Pocono Summit, PA 18346

Gift
8/13
MJ

i 13940624   JG

For the women and men who lost their lives.
For the ones who lived to tell their stories.

Nothing good ever comes of violence.
Martin Luther

Praise for
THE SUNDAY MORNING WIFE

"Being in the church never made any one a Christian. Pamela Rice proves this in her debut novel, The Sunday Morning Wife. From page one, Rice opens this novel with a devastating truth about domestic violence. First Lady Yolanda Clark is about to embark on a journey where she has do decide what really comes first in her life, her abusive husband or her own health and happiness. This is a must read novel for readers of every genre."

~ Linda R. Herman, Author of *Cost of Our Affairs*

"Ms. Rice's main character takes you on a heartfelt journey that will have readers looking deep inside their souls. Yolanda is the most realistic and charming female character I've read in years."

~ Stacy-Deanne, Award-Winning
Mystery and Suspense Novelist

"Pamela Rice offers an inside view into the lives of women who silently endure unspeakable violence. This book makes you look at every woman you pass in church, wondering if they are a victim. I can see this book being optioned to the big screen- this is a story that has to be told!"

~ Anthony "Tony" Grant
Singer, Actor, Producer, Writer

ACKNOWLEGEMENTS

I have to thank God first. I know that thanking God seems to be the norm for authors, entertainers, athletes, and many others. (That, along with going to Disney World.) I am truly sincere when I say that I thank God for all that He has done. This road has been one of the hardest I've experienced, but I wouldn't take nothing for my journey now!

To Elissa Gabrielle: Where do I begin? You have given me a chance, and that's all I ever wanted. Thanks for believing in my work. I am indebted to you forever. You are a beautiful lady, inside and out. I am so grateful to be a part of the Peace In The Storm publishing family! Thanks mami!

To my husband Wayne: You have been a strong tower for me. Whenever I wanted to give up, you were always there to encourage me to keep going. You are such a sweet, humble man, and I am honored to call you my helpmeet. You have made so many sacrifices for me and I'll love you forever! I can't imagine life without you…

To Anthony, Joseph, and Alanna: You all are what make me tick everyday. The love I have for you cannot be explained. I thank God everyday that he has blessed me with beautiful, loving children. Love you guys!

Mom and Dad: How can I say thanks for all the life lessons that you both have taught me? We never had much growing up, but yet you both taught me to be a giver. I still don't have much, but I am a giver. A closed hand gains no wealth. I love ya'll!

Princess: Where do I begin? I love you so much! You are my best friend, my confidante, my sister. I can tell you anything and know that you will not judge me. Carlton, Hannah, Sydney, Myla- love you all too!

Clote Rice: You accepted me as your daughter from day one, and I will never forget that. I Love you MaMa, and all your children, grandchildren, etc.

Believer's Fellowship: Pastor Allen and Mrs. Karen, you all are so real! Thanks for your support and love. Thanks to the church family- We are a small church with a big heart!

To my family and friends: Our family is so large! There is no way that I could list everyone. Thanks so much for your support and love. I am eternally grateful. The Foster's and Wilkins' rock!!!

Tracie Fowler, Daffenty Jones: What can I say? Both of your middle names should be dependable, because that what you are! If there is a need, you all supply! Thanks for your love.

Marcella Makins: Thanks for trying to push me to sing! Love you girl! I'm glad you think I can sing!

Latoya S. Watkins: Many thanks to you my fellow Peace sister! I am so appreciative that you took time out of your busy schedule to edit my book. Love Ya Sis!

Tony Grant: Even though we were reconnected through the tragic death of a friend, there was purpose. Thanks for all that you have done. I asked you for help, and you did not hesitate to give it to me. Thanks for your kind heart! Love Ya!

Drake Hill: Where should I start? Thanks for offering your resources and time. You are a long time friend, and your dad was my first boyfriend. (This is a joke, everyone) Thanks for introducing me to Peron. Love Ya!

Peron Long: Thanks for helping a sister out! I asked you so many questions and you were so patient with me. You are an awesome writer and I am truly a fan. Love Ya!

CHAPTER 1

Yolanda Clarke struggled to stand, but her wobbly knees failed her. She grabbed the bottom right corner of her white Laura Ashley comforter, sprinkled with pink handmade roses, and now her blood. Knuckles burning from grasping tightly, she pulled herself onto the bed.

Her husband Timothy bellowed out orders and commands in the background. "Get up! Don't turn your back on me when I am talking to you." His arms were swinging wildly; his face was contorted into that of a madman. Yolanda hardly recognized Timothy; a handsome man who everyone said resembled Harry Belafonte. She remembered when she first met him how his smooth brown skin, soft hair, chiseled chin, and twinkling eyes caught her attention. She closed her eyes and tears fell.

Yolanda wondered how she had arrived at her current state of hell, tormented day and night by someone who pledged, in front of God and man, to love her forever. Before her thought process could be finished, Timothy grabbed her by her hair, pulled her off the bed like a rag doll, and dragged her into the closet.

"Timothy, please, no!" Hoping her weight would keep him from shutting the door, she pressed her body against it.

"Timothy, please stop!" She pleaded with her husband to have mercy.

The door flew open forcefully, and Timothy kicked Yolanda so hard it sent her flailing against the back wall of the closet with a thud. Yolanda's mouth filled with blood and she screamed in pain, not knowing which hurt worse; almost biting her tongue in half, or the kick in the stomach. Praying his savage attack had ended, Yolanda curled into a fetal position. Timothy slammed and locked the door. Her whole body ached, and it felt like someone had hit her in the stomach with a two by four. She struggled to catch her breath, while also trying to suppress the cough in her throat. Yolanda cried quietly, her eyes struggling to become acclimated to the blackness surrounding her. The salty tears and nasal drainage trickled in and around her mouth, mingling with the blood from her tongue.

"I hate to treat you like this Yolanda, but it's really all your fault! All you have to do is just conform to the person that I am trying to mold you into. I have given you every pointer I know on how to be a perfect wife. I have printed out material for you to read, I have purchased books, and I have even sent you to workshops. But, you still don't seem to get it. You still don't know how to be a Proverbs thirty-one wife."

Yolanda could hear that Timothy's voice had dropped a couple of octaves, and surmised that he had calmed down a little—a good sign for her.

"And, this is the second time I've spoken with you about your loud breathing." Timothy continued, "I work hard everyday, and when I go to bed, I expect to have a little peace and quiet, without someone breathing heavily down my neck. It's probably because you are so fat. Not one of my friends' wives is as big as you. If you wonder why our sex life is suffering, look in the mirror. Your body disgusts me." Timothy's voice sounded like it was beginning to crack from the yelling earlier. "I'm still a man, and a man has needs, Yolanda. So, I sleep with you from time to time, just to satisfy my manly desires, but I don't like to. By the way, being overweight is also why you can't get pregnant. If you would read something besides your shrink magazines, you would know that."

Yolanda wished that Timothy would die, and wanted to kill him herself. At that moment, being intimate with him was the last thing on her mind. She stared into the darkness, watching the light that crept in under the door fade in and out as Timothy paced. Although she wanted to scream, she knew better. Any outburst would have unleashed a new round of brutality from Timothy. The first blow to her ear earlier certainly came out of nowhere. The pain was so intense it felt like someone was holding a fire poker against it. Yolanda was horrified when she felt the blood trickling down. The next blow was a tooth-rattling uppercut to the jaw. The final kick did her in. Even if she'd had the courage to fight, which she didn't, it was all over after the final blow. All she could do was listen and pray that the ordeal was over.

"And don't try to talk about how tall you are, or that you are big boned! You are just fat, F-A-T, and you need to lose some weight. You are going to learn to be a respectful, submissive, lady-like, slim wife, even if I have to beat you everyday. The choice is yours."

Yolanda waited anxiously, afraid to breathe, hoping that Timothy would not open the door. Yolanda was perplexed at how the little things seemed to set Timothy off. Still holding her breath, she strained her ear, listening intently. When she didn't hear a sound, she exhaled sharply. Even though she was locked in a closet like a caged animal, Yolanda felt safe, finding peace in the darkness. The hem of her nightgown became a washcloth to soak up the blood from her tongue and her ear. All too soon, the click of the key in the lock signaled that she could come out of her supposed prison and get ready for church- after she cooked breakfast. Yolanda crawled out of the closet, dreading standing, knowing with certainty that a headache was on the way. She yearned to sleep, but it was now six in the morning, and the first service started at nine. She walked gingerly to the shower, and stepped in, allowing the warm water to flow over her body. She winced as she touched her ear, which felt grotesquely swollen, and gently washed the dried blood away as best she could. As she washed her abdomen, she noticed the large bruise right above her navel.

Her body was full of old and new bruises, and Yolanda cried as she looked at the map of shame covering her body.

After cooking a full breakfast, which consisted of grits, scrambled eggs, toast, and turkey bacon, Yolanda knocked on Timothy's office door to let him know his breakfast was ready. She went upstairs to get dressed. Timothy would usually eat breakfast in his office downstairs on Sunday mornings, and wouldn't come out until it was time to leave for church. She was safe for the moment. I hope you die in there, she thought.

Like many Sunday mornings before, Yolanda methodically went through her routine of putting on her makeup and church face, taking care to hide her battle scars. Her appearance was meticulous. The peach St. John crinkle knit suit fit her to perfection, and the Louboutin pumps topped the ensemble off. Once she arrived at church, Yolanda made sure that her "Amen's" were on cue, and that she appeared enthusiastic during the sermon. During the service, Timothy had the gall to draw attention to her.

"I want everyone to look at the beautiful Mrs. Clarke. Isn't she a ray of sunshine today? She puts the pep in my step. She's my apple dumpling, my sweetie pie. I tell her everyday how lucky I am to be married to her." Timothy continued to brag to the church about what a wonderful wife she was, and the congregation erupted in "Amen's" and go-on-Pastors. Timothy looked Yolanda squarely in the eye.

"You really got a hold on me, baby." Yolanda smiled. She knew that not smiling meant another altercation once she got home. But inside, she was nauseous, and hoped Timothy would stop his charade, and let everyone see him for the devil he was. No one would ever believe that Pastor Timothy Clarke was a wife beater.

CHAPTER 2

Tired after a long Monday counseling scheduled and unscheduled patients, Yolanda made a pit stop at Publix to pick up a few dinner items. She had planned on making spaghetti, garlic bread, and salad for dinner; something quick and easy. As she walked down the pasta aisle, one of the couples she counseled came to mind. Brian and Tara had been married for five years and Brian had beaten her behind for four. He had certainly drained her today. He would not even participate at all, just shrugging his shoulders at every question that she asked. When she asked him why he continued to abuse Tara, he just sat there. At times, Yolanda felt compelled to jump up out of her office chair and slap him. She realized that the Bible taught Christians to draw people with loving kindness, and to never call them hurtful or derogatory names, but some of them just pushed you to the limit. Being saved, fire-baptized, and Holy-Ghost filled didn't stop her from wanting to strangle people sometimes. Yolanda knew that God was still delivering her in that area. Her tolerance was very low for people who hurt others willfully. Brian had a big, pockmarked frog-face, even bigger nose and lips, and he was the color of a maize crayon. He never looked anyone in the eyes; he just cast nervous glances their way from time to time. He always seemed restless and jumpy, like he was waiting for something to happen.

Yolanda thought about an occurrence in the past when Tara had been subjected to a brutal beating the day before one of their scheduled sessions. Tara walked in after a visit to the emergency room with two black eyes, several bruises, and a broken clavicle. Yolanda didn't even ask what excuse she gave to the emergency room staff on that occasion. She pulled Tara aside and told her to leave him, but Tara just looked mortified as if Yolanda was the one beating her instead of Brian.

Yolanda still wondered how she could have married Timothy, and ended up at BrightStar Tabernacle, working for free. She tried to recall a sign; something that would have alerted her to his ways, but failed. Timothy was always the model boyfriend and fiancé, no holds barred. The first two years of marriage were great. He used to bring her a bouquet of flowers every Friday. They weren't expensive, but the thought made Yolanda feel like a queen. The head to toe massages, the breakfast in bed, and the weekly lunch dates used to make her feel special. Then, out of nowhere, all hell broke loose. Yolanda would never forget the day. It was a dreary Saturday, and Timothy's phone kept ringing incessantly, to the point of annoyance. He was in the shower and could not hear it ringing. Tired of the noise, Yolanda answered the phone, only to have the caller hang up. When Timothy entered the bedroom, Yolanda told him what had transpired. He yelled at her, scaring her witless. Until that very moment, Timothy had never even raised his voice to her. Then he slapped her, telling her to never answer his phone again, along with a long list of other rules. And so the violence started. Yolanda was still searching, seeking, wondering what went wrong, her mind unable to comprehend the change in his behavior.

Yolanda spent her days counseling parishioners in every area, from sexual abuse, marital problems, to multiple personality issues. She still regretted the day that she passed up a job with the FBI performing personality profiling for serial killers to marry Timothy. The months and months of interviews, rigorous training, background checks, and subtle mind games, all wasted on a dream that turned into a nightmare. Although she truly cared for her clients, she disliked the church folk who thought that Pastor Timothy Clarke walked on water. Yolanda was repulsed by the women who were always in his face, flirting with him, especially Vicki, his secretary. They would bat their eyes at him, or "accidentally" brush up against him. More than anything, she had an aversion to the fact that her husband was just like Brian, physically abusive with no plans to change.

As Yolanda passed a couple in the grocery store, she stopped and stared at them. Yolanda noticed the way the man gently brushed the small of the woman's back, and let his hands slide down knowingly over her body. The lady looked into his eyes and smiled, welcoming his touch. At that very moment, she felt utterly and completely alone. The thought of someone touching you in love instead of anger was foreign to her. Yolanda felt her body warming, longing and yearning for love.

Yolanda scanned her spaghetti at the checkout, inserted cash into the machine, grabbed her change and receipt, and headed towards the door. She felt someone staring at her and looked up and saw what she thought to be a superbly polished chocolate specimen with the prettiest set of white teeth she'd ever seen smiling at her. His skin was pure mocha, and he had to be at least six-five. Yolanda blushed, willing herself to look and walk away, but she couldn't. She noticed his smooth bald head, well groomed mustache and goatee. He was wearing a perfectly tailored gray suit with a crisp pink shirt and cuff links. His nails were clean and perfectly groomed, and he was not wearing a ring on every finger. Yolanda could not stand seeing a man with dirty nails. One of her pet peeves, it was the first thing she noticed. She understood perfectly well that some jobs required getting dirty, and that was excusable. But, to be dressed to the nines and have dirty nails was totally inexcusable. Yolanda also felt like a ring on every finger was total overkill.

The stranger walked towards her, still smiling. He extended his hand. "Hi, I'm Andre Hunter, and you are?"

"Mrs. Clarke," She completed for him.

Yolanda felt the electricity as soon as she placed her hand in his, and jerked her hand away quickly.

"Well Ms. Clarke, do you have a first name?" He asked.

"That's Mrs. Clarke, and my first name is Yolanda."

"Who's the lucky guy?" Andre was waiting for an answer.

"Oh...I'm married to Timothy Clarke, pastor of BrightStar Tabernacle." Get it together, girl. Stop staring, she thought.

"He is one lucky man."

"You think so?" She asked with raised eyebrows.

"Yes, I certainly do. Yolanda, please forgive me for being so forward, but would you like to have dinner with me sometime?"

Yolanda had never once thought about stepping out on Timothy, but with the physical, mental, and emotional abuse at home, she contemplated it. Also, the undeniable chemistry between the two of them was unmistakable. The air was filled razor sharp electric currents that sliced them both to the core. I would love to have dinner with you, she thought. Yolanda imagined herself wrapped in Andre's arms, hypnotized by his smile. He leaned in slowly to whisper in her ear. The sound of Andre's voice brought her back from her quick daydream.

"No answer is a good answer, I guess. Why don't you just give me your number? We can start slow, get to know each other, and then maybe we can have dinner together someday." He waited for her reply.

"Sure. I guess that would be alright. Friends. Nothing more, nothing less." Even though it was totally out of character for her, Yolanda obliged and gave him her business card. She couldn't deny her attraction to Andre, and sensed that he picked up on it also. He offered her his business card also, and Yolanda looked at the glossy black and gold embossed card that read Andre Hunter Enterprises, LLC.

"What kind of business do you own?"

"I own a Tele-Communications Company. Are you looking to make a career change?"

"No, not really. Just curious, that's all."

Yolanda made direct eye contact with Andre. "Goodbye Andre." She located her keys, and pointed them toward her navy blue Lexus SC 400 Limited Edition to access the remote ignition. As she walked towards her car that was located directly behind her, she wondered if Andre was watching her walk away. Her heart began to flutter. When the doors didn't unlock, Yolanda clicked the remote entry again. She figured the battery must have been dead and walked over to the car and inserted the key. She turned the key, and the car still didn't unlock. Frustrated, Yolanda let out an audible sigh. She heard Andre laughing.

"What's so funny?" She questioned, almost offended.

"Why are you trying to get into my car?"

For a minute Yolanda looked dumbfounded. She looked around and noticed her car on the next row with the BrightStar tag on the front. She blushed and laughed.

"The dealer sold me this car as a "one of a kind" original." Yolanda chuckled softly and walked to her car.

"Mrs. Clarke, It was nice meeting you."

Yolanda smiled again as she put her bags in the car. "Lord, help me keep my mind stayed on thee." She mumbled as she got into her car.

Yolanda clicked the garage door opener and pulled inside the garage. Timothy had beaten her home and was probably inside taking a shower to prepare for dinner. Timothy getting home before her was rare. Yolanda grabbed the grocery bag and headed inside to the kitchen. She washed her hands and retrieved a jar of Prego from the pantry and placed it on the countertop, and gathered all of her other ingredients and began to assemble the spaghetti sauce. The recipe called for lots of crushed garlic and parsley sautéed in olive oil, Italian seasonings, a pinch of sugar, and then the Prego. She was using her late Auntie Louise's recipe.

Louise was Yolanda's favorite aunt. She was a large woman, who looked like she was made of steel. She always wore her jet black hair straight back and loose. Yolanda never knew for sure, but thought that her aunt weighed at least three hundred pounds. But, that didn't seem to bother the people who came back time and time again, seeking her services. She taught Yolanda how to cook everything. She owned a catering business, which was very successful, and catered a plethora of functions. Aunt Louise was just as comfortable preparing a chitlin' and fish fry dinner with all the sides as well as catering an elegant eight course meal for the mayor. She knew how to "spare no expense" and she also knew how to shop on a "nickel and dime." The spaghetti sauce was a shortcut recipe she learned when she did not have the ingredients to make the homemade sauce that usually simmered for hours. This secret sauce fooled everyone--every time. People always came back for more of what they thought was authentic.

Yolanda was the only niece of her childless Auntie, so when she died, she left Yolanda, her entire estate, which totaled almost a million dollars. Yolanda was very careful that she spent the money wisely. She hated Timothy more every time he took money for the church, which was often. She wished she'd never opened a joint bank account with him.

Yolanda's mother couldn't even boil water. Her grandmother Mabel had lived with them as long as Yolanda could remember and cooked breakfast, lunch, and dinner. There was bacon, sausage, eggs, grits, and biscuits for breakfast every morning. Yolanda missed lunch during the week because she was stuck at school, but dinner was a schedule that was the same every week. Sunday started out the week with fried chicken, rice and gravy, green beans or collards, biscuits and cornbread and whatever other vegetables were available. Sunday was also the day for dessert. There was always pound cake, peach cobbler, blackberry cobbler or sweet potato pie, or sometimes a combination. Monday was leftovers. Whatever was left over was what you ate, period. Grandma Mabel did not cook dinner on Monday because she used to go play bingo. Bingo night was a big deal for her and she rested all day so that she could have her "wits about her" as she would say, referring to her concentration. Friday was fish night. Yolanda loved Fridays. She would get in the kitchen and help her Grandma prepare the fish. They would wash it in the sink, season it well, and take it outside to fry in a huge cast iron pot. Grandma would cook enough fish for an army. She would serve coleslaw, hushpuppies, and French fries along with the fish. She would sell the plates for two or three dollars to make some extra cash for the family. Saturday, they would usually eat sandwiches or whatever they could scrounge up. This was the schedule for every week. If you did not like what was cooked, then you did not eat. Grandma would not have any waste in the house. That is how Yolanda learned to eat so heartily.

Yolanda heard Timothy coming down the stairs and snapped back to reality from her warm memories.

"What's up fat girl? What's for dinner?" Yolanda ignored him, and started to set the table. He stormed over to her and hovered so close to her that she could see his nostrils flaring. Timothy jerked the plate out of her hand, and threw her up against the wall.

"I said what's cooking, Yolanda? Are you deaf or something? You better answer me when I'm talking."

"Spaghetti," she said in a barely audible voice.

"Does the baby want her pacifier?" he asked when the tears began to roll down her cheeks. Yolanda despised when he patronized her, but felt helpless. She hoped he wouldn't make her suck the pacifier today like he'd done so many times in the past. It was so humiliating to walk around the house for hours with a pacifier stuck in her mouth. Seeing the pleasure that it gave Timothy always left her feeling dismayed.

Timothy continued to throw a barrage of degrading names at her while eating. Yolanda finished dinner without a word and got up from the table. She moved deliberately, not wanting to set Timothy off. Yolanda gathered her eating utensils and glass and placed them into the dishwasher. Yolanda went upstairs to the bedroom, pulled back the comforter and plopped down on the bed, with a million thoughts running through her head. Why do I continue to let him treat me like this? Why does Timothy feel that he must control every aspect of my life? It's probably all my fault anyway. Things would probably be better if I lost weight, learned to obey the rules, and tried harder to become the person that he wants me to be.

Yolanda heard Timothy coming up the stairs. She knew it wasn't over. "In order to be the head of the church; I have to be the head of my own house. It's already hard to be a pastor now days with the lack of commitment and murmuring among the believers. I don't need any resistance from you. That is probably why we have been married ten years yet still childless." Timothy paced around the bed. "You need to learn how to submit, relax and stop stressing over the little things so that your womb will receive the gift that God wants to bless us with." Yolanda wanted to tell him that if he would truly and completely satisfy her, and extinguish the unquenchable fire inside, then her womb would receive a million gifts from God.

Yolanda knew that it had been a couple of months since they'd been intimate, and she thought intimacy may sooth his anger towards her. She was desperate, willing to try anything to stop the violence, so she prepared herself for romance. Although she hated his abusive ways, in some strange way, part of her still loved him. She reasoned that if she would just keep praying, God would answer her prayers, and the abuse would stop.

Yolanda emerged from her walk-in closet wearing a black bustier, thigh high stockings, black thongs, and four inch heels.

"Who are you supposed to be? You look like Miss Piggy. You need to get somewhere and sit down and throw that mess in the garbage can. Get out of my face. You repulse me, walking in here looking like a tramp."

Yolanda was crushed, and wondered when a size ten became fat. She retreated to the bathroom, took off the lingerie, and threw it into the wastebasket. Yolanda could still hear Timothy laughing at her, calling her names.

"You need to do something about those inverted nipples, too. Maybe that's one reason you can't get pregnant. Those things are definitely not normal."

Timothy always had an excuse as to why she couldn't get pregnant. Maybe if he could ever quench the fire burning inside…. She walked to her dresser and grabbed a cotton nightgown, tears still flowing.

"I thought the lingerie was sexy, but tasteful, Timothy. We are a young couple, and I just thought that a little spice in the bedroom would keep things lively. I bet a lot of men would love to see me in that outfit."

At that moment, Timothy jumped out of the bed and stood so close to Yolanda that she could feel his breath on her face.

"You better never let me hear you talking about another man looking at you. If I even think you are thinking about it, I will kill you."

Timothy walked away, and Yolanda stood motionless with her mouth open. Yolanda tried to wipe the tears away, but the gates had already opened. She knew that death had to be better than the life she was living, and wished that everyone could see her husband for the monster he really was, instead of who he pretended to be. Yolanda despised Timothy for the way he treated her, but she still could not deny what she craved-intimacy and the human touch.

CHAPTER 3

The morning sun slid through the plantation shutters in the bedroom and Yolanda stirred slowly, waking up to a new day. Timothy had already left, and she breathed a sigh of relief. Yolanda had made it a whole week without a beat down, and she was ecstatic. The verbal insults had not subsided, but she figured she couldn't have everything her way. Yolanda showered and dressed, then put on a figure hugging white pantsuit, and a navy blue silk shirt that was accented with white polka dots. She slid into her four inch blue and white Italian leather pumps, which put her right at six feet, and looked at herself in her full length mirror. Her flawless caramel skin, slanted, cat-like eyes, and full lips made her look exotic. Her dad always said her eyes could pierce a man's heart and soul. Too bad they couldn't pierce Timothy's... Yolanda had coke bottle curves, her breasts didn't sag; she was a full C cup, and she didn't have one stretch mark on her body. If only my nipples weren't inverted...

Yolanda drove to work, thinking about her upcoming getaway with Timothy. Even though he had treated her terribly the week before, he was a little better this week. She thought about their upcoming trip. They hadn't been on vacation in ten years, since honeymooning in Hawaii. But, Timothy promised an overnight trip, and that was a start. Yolanda was ready to get as far away from church folk as she could. She loved God, but the people at church really rattled her sometimes. She always tries to give her all, but it never seemed like enough to satisfy anyone at church. Yolanda felt as if she wasn't good enough for the people, because no matter what she did, it never seemed right, unlike Timothy- who could do no wrong. They worshipped the ground he walked on.

Although Timothy's treatment was deplorable, Yolanda was still willing to try anything to turn their relationship around. She wasn't ready to fully give up on Timothy just yet. The vacation destination was a small chalet in the North Carolina Mountains, near the Biltmore House called Biltmore Chateau. Yolanda spent weeks searching the internet, trying to find the perfect spot. When she viewed the numerous pictures of the chateau online, she knew it was the place. With its romantic overtones Yolanda thought the chalet could awaken the deadest marriage. She fell in love with the waterfalls and greenery that surrounded the chalet. Also, the three light spa meals served daily didn't sound too shabby either. She could eat healthy meals and not have to worry about watching her caloric intake, and Timothy would approve of the light fare.

Yolanda headed to the kitchen to grab a yogurt drink. She craved an egg McMuffin from McDonald's, but Timothy would have a fit if he knew she ate fast food. He had her on a strict regimen. That meant exercising at least five days a week, eating right, and staying away from sweets. All those rules, and he still called her names. He wanted her to look good for him, but didn't want anyone to notice. Yolanda sipped her yogurt as she passed McDonald's. She refused to look too long or she would lose the battle to temptation. *Out of every temptation God prepares a way of escape...* She turned onto highway two ninety five and drove five miles to BrightStar.

As she made the left turn to go up the long, winding drive, she couldn't help but smile when she saw the beautiful edifice. It was a majestic brick sanctuary that seated about six thousand people. The windows were stained glass that told the story of Jesus' birth all the way up to his resurrection. Inside the sanctuary, the walls were painted in a soft lilac with white trim, while the carpet was a deep purple. The chandeliers hanging from the ceiling and sconces on the sidewalls cast soft light over the pews. Timothy said the purple and gold stood for royalty. Yolanda understood the symbolism, but for her, it was a place of refuge and peace. She would go in many times and just lay on the altar, just to talk to God. Yolanda would lay there for hours, asking God to purify her, make her whole, and to help her be a good First Lady and wife, so that the abuse would subside.

Yolanda walked through the side door toward her office. Mary, her receptionist was at her desk and greeted her with a warm smile.

"Hello, First Lady, how are you this morning?"

"I'm fine and how are you?"

"I am blessed and highly favored, thank you. Your coffee is on your desk." Yolanda thanked Mary as she walked into her office. The large rainbow mural that greeted her everyday was a reminder that God keeps his promises. Yolanda said a quick prayer asking God to help her give favorable and Godly advice, and to use her for His will. She sat down at her Ethan Allen desk, took a sip of coffee, looked over the day's appointments and cleared some paperwork out.

Yolanda noticed that Mary had penciled Tara in at two o'clock. She rubbed her temples and was unsure why Tara would be coming in again today after she saw her yesterday. God had to know that she was glad for her degree in Psychology from the University of South Carolina. She was a firm believer in having a true counselor's viewpoint, along with wisdom from the Lord, in order to handle the people that she dealt with everyday, especially Brian. She tried to like him, but it was hard. But, her dislike for Brian didn't stop her from praying for him. He needed to accept deliverance in Yolanda's opinion.

"Mrs. Clarke, your eleven o' clock appointment is here." Mary's upbeat voice rang out through the intercom.

"Thanks send her in please, Mary." Yolanda took a sip of the bottled water she grabbed from her fridge between sessions. Her mouth always became parched after talking so much in the counseling sessions, and she usually drank four or five bottled waters a day. She was sure Timothy would be happy because the water helped to keep her weight stable.

Amy Evans opened the door and walked in with a smile on her face. She was a pecan tan girl with huge oval eyes, and the longest eyelashes Yolanda had ever seen. Yolanda always told her if there was a prototype for Bambi's eyes, she was it. She had a small nose and full pouty lips; the kind people pay money to get. She had a short-cropped hairdo that suited her so well and framed her beautiful face. She wore a pair of white Capri pants and a yellow crop top and white Reeboks.

"So, First Lady Clarke, how are you today?" Amy chirped.

"I am fine Amy. You seem pretty happy today." Yolanda responded. "Have a seat and we will get started. Would you like something to drink?"

"No, thanks."

"Well, what have you been doing and how is the twelve step process coming along?" Yolanda asked. Yolanda had given Amy a booklet that she had written called Twelve Steps to Healing using Biblical Doctrine.

Yolanda remembered when it all started:

Amy's stepfather John, started sexually abusing her when she twelve years old. The saddest part was that her stepfather was a deacon in the church. Even worse was that Amy's mother was a deaconess in the church and accused Amy of trying to steal her man. Her stepfather strolled in after work one evening. "Cynthia, has Amy started having periods yet? "You keep asking me that. Why do you want to know?" "Because, I need to protect her from the knuckleheads by telling her about the "birds and the bees". They can smell blood on a young girl, just like a female dog in heat. I just want to make sure she doesn't end up pregnant." "Well, as her mother, I think this is something that I should handle. It's embarrassing to talk to a man about something so personal." "Do you want her to be embarrassed or pregnant?" Cynthia reluctantly told John when Amy got her first period and that's when the abuse began. He knew that if he molested her when her cycle was on, there would be no questions.

One night after everyone had gone to sleep, John entered Amy's room and closed the door. "Amy you are becoming a woman now and I need to talk to you about what to expect from boys. He sat down on the bed beside Amy and planted a kiss on her forehead. Amy felt awkward because he had never shown any signs of emotion towards her at all.

"This conversation is private and I need you to trust me, because all little girls have to go through this process to become a woman. How much bleeding have you had? Amy was so shocked and taken aback by his forthrightness that she began to tremble, mumbling under her breath. She was so embarrassed and kept looking for her mother to come in and rescue her. He draped his arm around her shoulder.

"Don't be so bashful. Now tell me, how much have you been bleeding?" Still, trembling, she just couldn't answer such a personal question.

"If you want to play dumb, I will just find out for myself. Remove your panties and gown." Tears began to well in Amy's eyes as she complied with her stepfather, wondering why he was so interested in something so personal and humiliating at the same time. Amy held back sobs and felt utterly humiliated at having a man look at something so personal.

"You know boys can smell blood on a girl." His eyes became dazed and fixed and Amy was so afraid that she didn't know what to do. She moved toward the door to get her mother, but John grabbed her wrist and held it in a death grip. He looked her dead in the face.

"Everything that goes on in this room is a secret. Everything." She knew he was the devil himself. At that very moment, she hated him so much she could have killed him. She remembered the story of David and Goliath from Sunday school, and knew one day she would have this giant's head. John removed a blade from his pocket. "You tell anybody and I will slit your throat, and kill your mama." John raped Amy. She muffled her screams of pain by placing her gown in her mouth. In the midst of the pain, Amy tried to figure out why her stepfather would do something so hideous. She knew he was supposed to be a deacon, and they were almost like preachers, or so Amy thought. She knew no one else in the world could ever go through what she was now enduring. Amy was so glad when John got off of her. She felt so dirty and could not wait to take a bath. John got up, used Amy's gown to wipe his private, put his clothes on and left without a word.

Amy lay trembling in the bed for hours until she was sure everyone in the house was asleep. Then she got up and went down the hall to the bathroom. She sat down on the toilet to relieve herself. After holding her urine for hours, she winced in pain as it burned her private. Amy felt like she had sat on a bowling ball and her whole bottom was sore. After she urinated, she turned to flush the toilet and screamed loudly when she saw the huge blood clots in the toilet and the bloodied toilet seat. Cynthia came running to the door. "Amy, unlock the door." Immediately, Amy began to panic, sure that John was going to kill her for screaming. "I'm okay, mom." Cynthia insisted she open the door. Visibly shaking, Amy opened the door slowly and allowed her mother to come into the bathroom. Cynthia noticed the clots immediately and assumed all the clots were from having her first period. She ran a warm bath for Amy and put some Epsom salt into the bathtub. "This will help with the cramps." Amy longed to tell her mother the truth, but couldn't risk John killing her mother. But deep inside Amy wondered if her mother knew. And the abuse continued.

Amy snapped Yolanda back to reality. "Mrs. Yolanda, did you hear me?" Amy dropped a bombshell and explained that after years of intensive counseling she was ready to take a break. Yolanda was caught by surprise because her bi-weekly Friday ritual was to counsel Amy. What will I do with my free time on Friday's now? Andre's beautiful smile immediately popped into her head. "Amy, I don't agree with your plan. I do not think you are ready to quit counseling. What you have been through is very serious. But, if you insist, you can come back in three months, then six months, and if everything continues to go well, come back for a yearly visit. I really want you to go home and think about the decision that you have made. Call me back next week and let me know what you decide. In the meantime, do you want to grab a bite to eat at the mall? I'm starving."

CHAPTER 4

Yolanda and Amy decided to go to Chick-fil-a and get grilled chicken sandwiches and diet cokes. Yolanda had not allowed herself to become close to many people at church, and although Amy was her patient, they had crossed the counselor patient line and become friends, with Yolanda serving as her mentor.

Vicki, who was still Timothy's secretary at BrightStar, used to be a close friend. Vicki was a perfect size eight, with breasts the size of small cantaloupes, a waist that you could wrap your finger around, and she had a firm round backside, or what some men called onion booty. She was a definite redbone through and through, with soft, golden honey hair splattered with blond highlights. Yolanda strolled into Timothy's office one day, forgetting her customary three knocks-and-wait-for-an-answer rule, and saw Timothy sitting on his desk with Vicki standing between his legs. Timothy looked her in the eyes and told her to never enter his office again without knocking, and that was the end of that conversation. Vicki looked back, smiled at her, and turned away. That was the end of their friendship. They passed one another in the church often after that episode, without as much as a glance. Even though Yolanda knew deep down they were having an affair, she didn't even want to graze the subject with Timothy. She already had enough problems with him. Sometimes you had to pick and choose your battles. Maybe this was another internal reason that Yolanda entertained the idea of having an affair with Andre.

After settling in at a table Yolanda and Amy both slurped hard on the Cokes, welcoming the refreshing coolness after being parched by the spring sun. They scanned the crowd to see if there were any familiar faces. People watching was one of Yolanda's favorite pastimes. All those classes in college had her wondering what made everyone tick. She was watching a kid lying in the floor throwing a temper tantrum when someone tapped her on the shoulder. It was Andre looking dapper in a navy blue Jeremy Schurr wide lapel suit with a white silk shirt buttoned down just enough for his sparse chest hair to peep out and tantalize Yolanda's eyes. Yolanda pursed her lips, swallowed hard to keep from drooling, and tried to regain her composure.

"Hello, Andre. This is my friend Amy. Amy, this is Andre."

"Hi, Yolanda, Hi Amy, it's nice to meet you." Andre made small talk and kept his gaze fixed on Amy the whole time. Even though she understood that she shouldn't be, Yolanda was raging with jealousy. She felt stupid to have even let herself be flattered by Andre's words in the Publix parking lot.

"Well, ladies. I guess I better get back to work. Again, it's nice to meet you, Amy. See you around, Yolanda." Yolanda remembered she had Andre's card in her purse and she would be sure to call him ASAP to give him a piece of her mind for flirting with her friend.

Amy scooped her face from the table. "Who is that fine brother, and how do you know him?"

"I met him in the Publix parking lot, and he only knows me as Mrs. Yolanda Clarke."

"Mrs. Yolanda, you need to hook a sister up." Amy smoothed her hair and checked her lipstick in her compact.

"Amy neither you or I know anything about Andre, and that's the best way to keep it." Yolanda managed to put on a happy face, despite being blatantly ignored by Andre, and suggested that it was time for her to go back to work.

When Yolanda arrived back at church, Tara was waiting for her in her office. Tara's left eye was badly swollen and her lips were busted up.

"Tara what happened to you?" Yolanda sputtered, dropping her purse on the wing chair.

"Did Brian do this to you? We are going to call the police again because he is going to kill you if you don't put a stop to the abuse. This has been going on long enough and God does not want us to be in a relationship with someone who is battering us everyday." *Why did I say us? I hope she didn't catch that.* Yolanda grabbed the phone and started to dial 911. Tara removed the phone from her hands and pleaded with Yolanda not to call.

"Mrs. Yolanda, I know that I have probably driven you crazy coming here battered and bruised year after year. But, Brian promised this would be the last time. It is really my fault anyway because I forgot to pick up his suit from the cleaners and you know some of the men from church are going to a Power Conference." Yolanda didn't even bother trying to interrupt Tara. She had learned from years of counseling that it was fruitless. She listened. "Anyway, he got mad and I told him to stop hitting me because I was pregnant. He stopped and sat down and cried. He told me he had always wanted to be a daddy, and that he would never hit me again. He promised Mrs. Yolanda, so you see; there is no need to call the police. I also wanted to tell you that we won't be coming to counseling anymore because he promised not to abuse me anymore."

"Have you lost your mind? What is it going to take for you to understand that this problem is not going to go away in one day? Men abuse women every day and say they will stop, but the fact of the matter is that not many at all keep their word. Brian has serious issues and he needs to continue counseling so that he can be free from the demons of abuse. You need to continue counseling so that you can be healed and understand that you do not have to be manipulated and controlled by a man. Tara, this is serious and you shouldn't take it so lightly." Yolanda was breathless, trying to explain to Tara but figured that she was fighting a losing battle, because little progress had been made in the five years that she had been counseling them.

"God will keep us from harm's way." Tara rubbed her belly.

"Honey, while God surely covers us, he wants us to have common sense to remove ourselves from situations that are demeaning and demoralizing. God wants to spread love, peace and joy and none of that was present in your relationship with Brian!" Yolanda felt the anger rising inside her, and reminded herself to remain professional.

"Mrs. Yolanda, when I married Brian, I pledged 'till death do us part, and I meant it!" Tara blurted through tears.

"Well Tara you know what, death is just around the corner for you, if you stay with Brian! He will not stop until he kills you, I can promise you that! I can pray for you night and day, but until you empower yourself to leave and know that his treatment of you is wrong; you will continue to be a victim. And bringing a small child into a volatile relationship is totally ridiculous!"

"Mrs. Yolanda, I have made my decision. Thank you for everything. Brian, me and the baby will be just fine." Tara walked out of the office. Yolanda sat down at her desk and cried, afraid to think of what was going to happen to Tara. Only God could help her now. Yolanda categorized their relationship as parasitic; one person feeding on the other until the parasite finally kills the host.

Too many thoughts were crowding Yolanda's brain and she couldn't think straight. She decided to call Andre. She opened her wallet and unzipped a small hidden zipper and retrieved Andre's card.

"Andre speaking" was all he said. After a five second silence, he added, "Mrs. Clarke, are you going to say anything?"

"How did you know that it was me?" Yolanda replied.

"The number is on your business card, remember?"

"What was that you pulled at lunch? I should have known you were a player, especially when you practically devoured Amy."

"Slow your roll, Mrs. Clarke. First of all, I am not a player. I used to be, but that lifestyle doesn't suit me anymore. I am looking for a smart sensible lady, and I think I found her. Secondly, I pretended to be interested in Amy so that she would not think that her First Lady had a man on the side. That wouldn't look to good for a Pastor's wife, now would it Mrs. Clarke?" His voice held more confidence than Yolanda was comfortable with.

"Andre, I am a married woman, and I will not be taken into your net and used and then tossed to the side, like a dirty rag."

"You missed a key word again, Yolanda."

"What are you talking about, Andre?" Yolanda tried unsuccessfully to squelch the steam rising inside again.

"You didn't say happily. That is the key word in a marriage, and for the second time you didn't say happily." Yolanda hung up on Andre without saying goodbye.

Yolanda grabbed her belongings, locked her office, and headed down the highway. She wondered what the enemy was up to by bringing this man into her life. God had to know better. Andre's smile haunted her thoughts and dreams. The chalet would be a great getaway to rid her system of Andre once and for all.

CHAPTER 5

Yolanda retrieved the luggage from the storage closet. She decided a garment bag and one small rolling suitcase would do for an overnight trip, and took the luggage up to the bedroom to pack. Wanting to make sure the trip would be one to remember, she purchased some nice modest lingerie from Victoria's Secret to set the mood. She also purchased some intimate warming liquid. She had never tried it, but she thought anything was worth a try to get her marriage back to what it once was.

Just as Yolanda finished packing the last of her travel accessories, Timothy walked into the bedroom.

"Timothy, I didn't hear you come in. How was your day?" Yolanda slid the warming liquid into a compartment in the garment bag and placed the luggage on the floor.

"It was good, Yolanda. Why are you packing?" He asked.

"Timothy, you know we are spending the night at Biltmore Chateau. Don't you remember?"

"Yolanda, I am sorry but I can't go tonight. Apostle Greene has called an emergency conference with all affiliates of the National Council. I am going to the airport now to pick him up, and we will be meeting at the chalet tonight up until tomorrow evening."

"Timothy you promised me that we would go. I know God has to be first in your life, but don't forget about your wife. I am always last on your list. I hardly ever see you! I feel like I am second- fiddle to everything and everyone else in your life. The people at church know more about you than I do!" Yolanda furiously kicked the suitcase.

"I just found out earlier today he was coming. Running a church is a full time job. I have thousands of people to try to steer in the right direction. You can be so selfish, Yolanda. I am trying to do God's will for my life, and you are whining about our relationship and a little trip. You need to stop living in the fairy tale world you've been in. Yes, you are second- fiddle right now, because I am investing all of my time and energy into the ministry."

"You let me go through all that, pouring myself out to you, when you knew we were not going? You couldn't call me BEFORE I packed all of these clothes?" Yolanda pointed to the garment bag and suitcase.

"Calm down Yolanda, you are making a mountain out of a molehill. We will go another time when I can fit you into my schedule."

"That's right Timothy; fit me into your schedule. If you can squeeze me in somewhere in your life, I will be very happy." Yolanda slung the garment bag and suitcase on the bed, and started unpacking, throwing her belonging everywhere.

"Amy decided that she was ready to stop counseling, which I have a problem with because I don't think she is ready. I scheduled her for a three month follow-up, just in case, and I can only hope that she will do well. Then, Tara came in and dropped the bomb, saying she was pregnant, Brian was not going to hit her anymore, and they were quitting counseling. So, as you can see, I need a break. I have got to get away to clear my mind. So you can go your way, and I will go mine."

Yolanda had never spoken back to Timothy, and she knew things would be bad for her, but she didn't care. Yolanda picked up the phone and started to make reservations at the new luxury hotel in town. Timothy walked over and yanked the phone from her, and struck her repeatedly about the face, chest and arms. Yolanda cowered in the corner of the bedroom, fighting off his blows as best as she could.

"I'm in charge here! You better remember your place! As long as I'm alive, I will make the rules! You got that, fat girl?" After having his say, Timothy packed the suitcase and left.

Yolanda grabbed the garment bag and tossed it across the bedroom, not even trying to minimize the anger building inside.

"I hope you die! I hope you die, Timothy! I hate you!" The screams came from the deep abyss of her core. The tears fell as she continued to throw the garment bag, wishing it was Timothy. Yolanda was so sick and tired of getting beaten; tired of Timothy telling her he was in charge. She fought the urge to kill him sometimes and only God kept her from doing so. Just thinking about him made her sick to her stomach.

Yolanda was still feeling the heat in her face as she threw the garment bag across the room once more. She sat on the bed and tried to gather her thoughts. The conversation she had with Timothy wouldn't leave her. He actually said that she was second-fiddle in his life. It was bad enough that he felt that way, but for him to actually say it; that was over the top. Yolanda thought about all the sacrifices she'd made for their marriage and ministry. She passed up a lucrative career. She passed up an opportunity to speak at the American Psychological Association's Annual Conference because it would have interfered with the Women's Conference at church. Don't even talk about dealing with the backbiting, husband-chasing women at church every Sunday. The ones who smiled in her face and tried to corner him every Sunday and offer to "help" him; the "call me if you need me" conversations. Yolanda wanted to burst their bubble and tell them nothing was going on at home, and to stop casting their goods at his feet.

Yolanda thought about how she and Timothy seemed to have it all. She drove a Lexus, he drove a Jaguar. They both owned custom clothing. They lived in a five hundred thousand dollar house in the suburbs that was always lit up inside. Still, it was not a home. Only love could make a home, and someone lording over every aspect of your life, and beating you senseless certainly wasn't love.

Feeling extremely lonely yet bold, Yolanda called Andre. She hoped he would talk to her, especially after she hung up on him.

"Hi, Mrs. Clarke. I've been waiting for your call."

"Hi, Andre. Listen, I want to apologize for hanging up on you. You hit a sore spot for me, and I reacted. I'm sorry."

"I accept your apology. Let me apologize also. I overstepped my boundaries. So, why don't we start over? Let's wipe the slate clean, and we can do that by going to dinner. Why don't you meet me at the West End in Greenville? Don't say you can't go, because I know your husband is not home. If he was, you wouldn't be calling."

"I'll have to think about it."

"What's there to think about? You're alone, I'm alone... Look, I promise we will have a private room and that no one will see you with me. I will go in the back entrance and wait for you in the private dining room. Trust me."

"This is certainly against my better judgment... I'll see you in an hour and a half."

Yolanda showered and dressed, and looked at her reflection in the mirror. She piled her makeup on, hoping to hide the bruises Timothy left behind, taking particular care to mask the bruise on her right cheekbone. Her pink silk dress with spaghetti straps complemented her caramel skin. Yolanda twisted her shoulder- length hair loosely in the back and secured it with two Chinese hairpins. She looked down at her perfectly manicured toenails that peeked out from her Jimmy Choo sandals, and decided she was ready.

As Yolanda stepped into the restaurant lobby, she was greeted with many stares of approval from men and women alike. She smiled warmly at her admirers and proceeded inside.

"Good evening ma'am. Do you have a reservation?" the hostess asked as Yolanda approached.

"Yes, in the private dining room."

Andre was waiting for her, dressed to the nines in all black. Yolanda's pulse quickened and she tried to place her attention anywhere else, rather than on Andre. She noticed the heavily upholstered chairs and white tablecloths with real flowers, dim lighting, and candles on the table.

"You look absolutely beautiful, Mrs. Clarke."

"Thanks, Andre. Please- call me Yolanda. And, if I must say, you look nice also."

Yolanda could see Andre's muscular physique, even in the suit, and she willed herself to stop staring. Andre walked closer to Yolanda. Her heart beat quickly, and she wondered what he would do when he got close to her. Andre pulled out her chair.

"May I?" Andre brushed his hand across Yolanda's shoulder as he seated her, sending chills down to her inner being. She had to find a distraction. Yolanda looked out of the window and observed that the restaurant overlooked a beautiful flower garden and waterfall. April showers had really made the May flowers beautiful.

Yolanda perused the menu given to her by the hostess and decided that she would have the grilled rib eye Chianti, garlic mashed potatoes with Gorgonzola cheese, and asparagus tips. The waiter recommended a glass of Chianti with the meal, and even though Yolanda had not tasted wine in years, she decided to have a glass.

As she waited for her meal she slowly sipped her wine, thinking about her marriage and her role as the First Lady of BrightStar. She felt stuck. Being married to a minister meant she always has to be on her best behavior, exemplifying a virtuous woman. She loved the Lord with all her heart, but people were beginning to make her life miserable. If someone from church saw her in the dress she had on, they would call her a floozy and probably want to kick her out of the church. But, she desired to be sexy sometimes; she wanted to show her feminine side. She firmly believed that you could be sexy and saved. Yolanda also wanted to relish in sexual pleasure and receive and give freely, but Timothy said that a virtuous woman carried her behavior to the bedroom as well. His thoughts lately were that wild, passionate sex was of the devil and wanted no part of it. There was only the missionary position and even that was not happening lately. Yolanda longed to experiment and let go in the bedroom, but Timothy told her that was her sinful nature rising and she must learn to suppress it. Andre brought Yolanda back to orbit.

"I'd give you a penny for your thoughts."

Yolanda smiled and took another sip of her wine.

The waiter placed Yolanda's and Andre's food in front of them and asked if everything was to their liking.

"Everything looks wonderful!" Yolanda looked at the meal, wondering how many calories it would set her back. After Andre blessed the food, Yolanda cut into the steak. It was medium well, just like she liked. She placed the juicy, tender steak in her mouth, enjoying the flavor. The potatoes and asparagus were delightful as well, and Yolanda also enjoyed the complimentary almond glazed croissants. She wondered what Timothy would say, seeing her eat such a fattening meal. Considering she only had a yogurt drink for breakfast and a chicken salad sandwich for lunch, she thought her dinner was well deserved. The waiter poured her another glass of Chianti.

"This will definitely be my last glass. It's been a long time." She was already feeling a little giddy and uninhibited.

"How are you enjoying your Mahi Mahi, Andre?"

"It's actually quite good."

"So, Yolanda, tell me about you. What makes you tick?"

"Well, I've been told I have a big heart."

"I don't want to know what other people think about you. I want to know how you feel about yourself." Yolanda was speechless. No one had ever asked her that. How could she answer that question?

"I'll get back to you on that." She and Andre continued to talk, and Yolanda felt special knowing that someone was actually listening to her, looking at her when she talked, and seeming to enjoy the conversation. She couldn't remember the last time Timothy complemented her, or even said anything nice to her for that matter.

After dinner, Yolanda decided that she would have dessert. She looked over the dessert menu and chose the crème brulee. Knowing that it was an indulgent dessert, she wanted something to indulge in tonight, and since it wouldn't be sex, dessert was the next best thing. Yolanda and Andre had an after dinner coffee, and ended up talking until midnight. The time flew by, and Yolanda couldn't believe it was so late. Yolanda was stuffed. She had never eaten that much food.

"Well, Andre, I really had a great time. Thanks so much for inviting me."

"Let me assure you, the pleasure was all mine." Andre kissed her gently, brushing his lips against hers. Yolanda responded, hungrily receiving everything his mouth was willing to give.

CHAPTER 6

The rain was falling steadily on the chalet rooftop, and it sounded like a soft rhythmic drum. It was Saturday morning, and Timothy nestled beside Vicki, resting his head on her breasts. He loved everything about her body. Her breasts were perfect, and they didn't creep him out like Yolanda's. He slid his hand down her thigh, signaling that he needed more attention.

Timothy disliked being married to Yolanda. However, her money made him feel powerful and important, and it was getting him closer to his mega church every day, and that's what kept him with her. Yolanda had the curves, the long black hair, and beautiful skin, but she just didn't do it for him. Yolanda was almost as tall as he was, and when she put on heels, she was a tad bit taller. Most of all, she didn't understand him. She was just his Sunday morning wife.

Timothy had never told anyone, but he used to see his dad beat his mother all the time. He loved his mother so much, and always felt too helpless to assert himself against the abuse his dad inflicted on his mother. His dad was a violent man, and when he was tired of using his mother as a whipping post, he would start in on Timothy. Timothy's mother made him promise he would never tell anyone about the abuse they endured. She also made him promise never to hit his wife. Timothy was easily able to keep the first promise, but the second one was hard to keep. Yolanda just made him so mad sometimes. Even though both his parents were dead, he still had pure hatred for his dad, and what he put his mother through on a daily basis.

When Timothy had night terrors about his dad, Yolanda was always the psychologist, asking him what was wrong and trying to analyze the situation. She could never just be a wife and hold him. But, if he had a bad dream when he was with Vicki, she slid her body close to his, and pressed herself tightly against him, holding him until he stopped shaking. She then proceeded to give him the most unselfish sex that he had ever had. Timothy wasn't delusional about Vicki. He knew that she did not love him, and it was all about his money, but she comforted him. Still, Vicki had a few things in her life that she needed to straighten out. He had tried to tell her several times that she needs to be saved, and she just laughed at him and told him that he had nerve to try to preach salvation to her when he was the biggest sinner of all. She always shut him down, telling him she did not want to hear it. Timothy tried once to control her with his hands, just like he did Yolanda, but after Vicki won the fight, he decided that he'd better not push her buttons. First, she kicked him in the groin, and when he leaned forward in agony, she kneed him squarely in the forehead. As he fell to the ground, writhing in pain, she kicked him repeatedly in the stomach, making sure the pointed toe of her stiletto made solid contact. She used the stiletto to step on his privates, sending intense pain signals to his brain. After she finished cursing, hitting, biting, punching, and screaming at him, he knew that she was a cat that could not be tamed. He later learned that Vicki grew up with six boys, and back then, it was her or them.

Timothy told Vicki about the plans for the day, and as long as shopping was involved, she would be fine. Timothy decided they would shop first, and then get deep tissue massages and mud baths at Asia, a spa they saw on the drive to the mountains, then come back and have lunch at the chalet.

THE SUNDAY MORNING WIFE

Timothy was irritated that Yolanda would not pick up the phone last night, but he was not going to let her ruin his day. Yolanda knew how to ruin a good mood, even when she was not around.

After multiple dreams of Andre's lips touching hers, Yolanda got up and made her bed, smiling the whole time. While she was in the shower, she tried to remember the sensation of Andre's lips against hers. After getting dressed, she decided to splurge for breakfast. Food was going to be her new best friend today, because Timothy was gone, and she could eat whatever she liked. She went to IHOP and dined on a platter of pancakes with ham, eggs, and a side of grits. No one was going to control her today, telling her what to do. She thought about her life and how sad it has become. How have I gone from a bright, vibrant, young lady to scared victim?

After breakfast, Yolanda decided to pay her parents, Walter and Lola Reed, a visit. Their relationship had been strained since she married Timothy. Yolanda had to admit that her father was right about him. He warned her that Timothy was a wolf in sheep's clothing, but Yolanda was in love and would not listen. Right before he walked her down the aisle, he told her that she could still back out.

Yolanda knocked at the door, waiting for an answer. Her mother opened the door and was surprised to see her.

"Hi, Yolanda, it's really good to see you." She gave Yolanda a tight squeeze. Yolanda entered and greeted her father, who was sitting in the den reading the newspaper.

"Hi, pumpkin. It's been a long time. How are things going?" Yolanda's father kissed her on the forehead and settled back in his chair. They made small talk, catching up on current events.

"So, is there a baby on the horizon anytime soon?"

"No mom, there is not. The way my marriage is headed; there will never be any children. You guys were right about Timothy. He is self –absorbed and so cynical." She started on an emotional tirade.

"I'm sorry for not listening to you, and I'm sorry for the time I spent away from you. I thought I was doing the right thing. I couldn't see the forest for the trees. Now my life is a mess."

Yolanda's mother comforted her. "Don't you worry honey, everything will be alright." Yolanda realized that although her parents disagreed about her choice for marriage, they still loved her. After getting on the path to reconciliation with them, Yolanda headed home, promising to visit more often.

Yolanda's phone rang for what seemed like the hundredth time, and she thought it was Timothy again. He had already left several threatening messages for her, wondering where she was. Even though she was deathly afraid of him, she couldn't keep living the way she was. She doubted that he was really with Apostle Greene, but she was too emotionally drained to care. Yolanda glanced at her phone and saw Andre's number.

"Hello."

"Hi beautiful, I just want to know if we are still going to get together on Sunday."

"Wild horses couldn't keep me away." Yolanda could hardly believe that she was being so verbal and straightforward, but she liked her newfound confidence. Andre gave her directions to his home and told her to meet him tomorrow after she got out of church.

Yolanda went into the house, changed into her swimsuit, and headed to the pool. She swam a couple of laps and sat on the stairs leading into the pool, taking a breather. She heard Timothy walking up and turned toward him. Before she could react, he grabbed her by the neck and repeatedly dunked her under the water, as she gasped for air.

"Why have you not answered my calls? Once again, I am the head of this house, and if I have to kill you to make you realize it, then so be it. One way or another, you will learn to submit." Timothy released Yolanda from his vice grip and towered over her as she panted, hoping that air would soon fill her lungs.

"Timothy, why are you treating me so bad?"

"Because, I can." Timothy walked away and turned around at the door. "Oh, I also took fifty thousand of your aunt's money to help with the additional parking at church. We were short on the fundraiser." Yolanda knew her money probably went to some woman, like Vicki, and she sat, still shaken, but angry. There was no way she could let this one pass.

"You mean to tell me that you won't let me hire a housekeeper, even though it's really my money, and I work FOR FREE at church, and you are spending money on a parking lot? Without consulting me?" Yolanda felt that she was inviting more trouble, but had to have her say. She was slowly growing weary of Timothy, his lies, and abuse.

"We agreed never to touch the account until we both were in agreement as to how the money would be spent." Yolanda was speaking in a high pitched shrill voice and tried to catch her breath. She walked over to him, and slapped him so hard that she thought she broke her hand. With the deadly strike of a cobra, Timothy wrapped his hands around her neck and pushed her down to the ground. Her lungs that were already pleading for air begged for mercy. Yolanda tried to scream, but nothing audible could escape because of the death grip that Timothy had on her. She looked up at Timothy with a look of panic and desperation, but all she received in return was a look of fierce anger. Yolanda saw the vein in Timothy's neck swell and realized that he was yelling at her. "Never hit me again!" was all she heard before she closed her eyes.

Yolanda woke on the couch, still in her swimsuit, shivering. At least Timothy brought her in the house this time, instead of leaving her outside. A massive headache was building and Yolanda felt like a candidate for the trephining process of long ago. Turning to the clock, tears welled in her eyes as she thought about the time she had lost. It was now eleven o' clock and she couldn't account for hours of her life. Yolanda began to sob quietly. How could Timothy keep treating her so badly? Yolanda closed her eyes and prayed. Even though her life was crazy, and spiraling out of control, she still made time to meditate, pray, and study every day. Yolanda realized that a shift was taking place in her life, and wondered if the shaking was from God- or the enemy.

CHAPTER 7

Yolanda opened her closet and walked in. It was Sunday morning and she had to find something to wear to church. She selected a pale pink suit from the closet. It was one many gifts Timothy had purchased for her, and she couldn't believe that he'd spent almost a thousand dollars on it. But, Timothy expected her to look her best every Sunday. He told her that if she was representing him, she had always better dress to impress, never looking shabby. Yolanda made sure that he approved what she was wearing every week, just to keep the peace.

Yolanda was so tired of having her life dictated. She continued to pray, asking God for help and strength. Her thoughts floated to Andre and what life could potentially be like with him. He seemed so kind and attentive to her every word. Yolanda figured he could really please a woman in bed- something she longed for. Her skin flushed, and her body became heated as she tried to dismiss Andre from her thoughts. *Sorry Lord, I know my mind should be on you right now, and my heart preparing for worship…* She was aware that she didn't even really know him, and he could be like the other men that tried to get next to her. Yolanda could tell easily that some men only wanted sex from her, and it was so apparent. Not necessarily the people on the street, but the preachers, deacons and other church folk. They disgusted Yolanda with their tired lines and clichés about their sexual prowess and staying power. She had heard every line in the book and never even once thought about giving herself to another man. But Andre sparked something deep down inside.

Yolanda dressed for church, not saying a word to Timothy. She could have easily killed him with one of her stilettos as he slept last night, just like Sisera killed Jael in the Bible, but she couldn't muster up the courage to do so. Yolanda tried to cover the bruises on her neck by wearing a black Hermes scarf with pink ladybugs, another one of Timothy's purchases, and topped the ensemble off with a pink hat.

Sunday morning services were a strain for Yolanda. She closed her eyes as the choir serenaded her with a song about being safe in the arms of Jesus. Even though the song was old, it was a timeless masterpiece. The person that wrote the song had been through some real trials and tribulations. Yolanda wiped the tears that welled in her eyes during the song, and adjusted the scarf around her neck, wondering if anyone could see her battle scars. There was a feigned interest in Timothy's sermon. Yolanda could not believe he had the nerve to preach about "Getting Your House in Order" after he tried to snuff out the last breath from her yesterday. Disgust rose in her belly and the stench moved to her throat. She tried to maintain a fake smile because the older women of the church always watched her like a hawk. She wanted to tell them that she could see them hunching one another in the sides and staring at her, trying to gauge her mood. The people at church felt that she didn't exactly fit the role of a First Lady, and they only tolerated her because they loved Timothy so much. They didn't think that she was active on enough boards at church, but Yolanda knew that she could not give her all to her patients if she served on any of the boards. They expected her to come to every meeting for each auxiliary, and when she didn't, she quickly became an outcast. She realized their smiles were made of plaster and that they truly despised her. She had caught several of them sneering at her before, and when she caught their attention, the sneers faded away like a gentle summer breeze on a hot day. So quick to dissipate that she really had to wonder if she imagined it. Yolanda wished that she could confide in just one of the elderly ladies, but she knew that they would never believe that Timothy was abusing her. She longed for someone to talk to and tell her troubles to.

Timothy was nearing the end of the sermon and it was time for him to crank it up. Yolanda looked in her periphery and saw Vicki sitting behind her. When Vicki noticed that Yolanda was looking, she jumped up and waved her arms, shouting exuberantly. Yolanda wanted to beat the hell out of her and Timothy, then tell everyone about the affair they were having. Timothy's voice rose and fell in crescendo with the organ chasing behind him, hot on his trails. Yolanda watched as the usual "shouters" fell in line with the organ, bodies pulsating to the downbeat. Sister Gerri fell into her routine of shouting out of her clothes, revealing a black lace camisole underneath her button down shirt. Her push-up bra barely kept her bosom from spilling out. The long split in her dress revealed black matching lace panties after she was "slain in the spirit" and fell to the floor. Yolanda watched in derision after the ladies took their cue to entertain the males and maybe a few females in their very own private peep show. Yolanda believed in the Holy Spirit, the five-fold ministry and spiritual gifts, but it wouldn't take a rocket scientist to figure out that the women were flesh bearers. The ushers performed their duties and covered everyone up. Of course Sister Gerri kept kicking her covering off, allowing the deacons that she just happened to fall in front of to catch another glimpse of her lacy undergarments.

Timothy ended the sermon and beckoned those who didn't know Christ to come to the altar. The rest of the service was a blur to Yolanda after getting caught up in the choir singing about how precious the Lamb of God was. The Holy Spirit took control and Yolanda rocked and cradled herself and spoke to the Father in a language that only He could understand.

After church, so many women commented on her scarf. They always seemed to notice when she wore something new. Yolanda had always thought scarves were kind of dorky, but now wondered if the women who wore them were hiding a secret like she was. Seeing remnants of Timothy's handprints on her neck when she awoke this morning really hit her hard and made her realize that the letter death was writing only needed a signature to be complete. She started to tell the inquiring women that she wore the scarf because her husband tried to kill her, but knew better. She tried to divert their attention away from her scarf by talking about the sermon that almost made her throw up.

After making her rounds to speak to other members of the congregation, Yolanda walked to her office and locked the door. She sat at her desk and removed a bottle of Excedrin migraine from her drawer and popped a couple, swallowing them dry. Yolanda needed to talk to someone about what happened, but could think of no one to confide in. If her auntie or grandmother were still alive, she could go to them. She could never tell her parents about the abuse, especially since they were just getting comfortable with each other again.

Yolanda opened her purse and pulled out Andre's card. She dialed the number and waited for him to answer.

"What does a brother have to do to get a phone call?" Andre answered, happy to finally hear from Yolanda. Andre gave directions to his home again.

"Go to the Twin Lakes Subdivision, turn right on Ashe Lane and my home is the fifth one on the right. One-five-five Ashe Lane. The garage door will be open; just pull in." Yolanda recited the directions out loud to Andre. She had to memorize the directions because she could not risk writing them down.

"I'll be there in about an hour. What kind of communications business are you in to have a home in Twin Lakes?" Yolanda asked, knowing that the older upscale community still cost a pretty penny to live in.

"We'll talk about that when you get here." She rose from her desk and entered her bathroom to freshen up. She adjusted the scarf around her neck, and brushed her teeth. She didn't want to offend Andre with bad breath. His mouth was like nectar, and she couldn't wait to drink.

As she touched up her makeup, Yolanda wondered how she would get away from Timothy without him being suspicious.

She decided to tell him she was going to put some fresh flowers on her grandmother's and auntie's graves. Timothy would not argue with that, because he knew she spent time keeping the gravesites nice and neat. He also knew she liked to go alone, because it gave her time to reflect and think. Yolanda would sit for two or three hours sometimes, just thinking about life and pondering her place in the world. Timothy went once, and after a three-hour stint of sitting and looking at graves, he'd had enough. He wasn't afraid, just bored. Yolanda realized that the graves only contained dust and bones, and that her auntie and grandmother were in heaven, but she found comfort there. Yolanda gargled with mouthwash and checked herself in the mirror once again. She walked out of her office and down the hall to Timothy's office. She tapped on the door using her secret code, and waited for him to answer. Yolanda thought it was crazy to have to knock on her own husband's office door, but was tired of getting nowhere asking why. Only after he answered did she open the door and step in.

His office was very conservative with a huge imposing desk made of oak. The walls were painted a dark blue that made the room look gloomy. Everything in the office was hard, and had rigid lines, with no softness anywhere. His chairs were hard burgundy leather that didn't give when you sat on them. He had one picture on his desk and it was a picture of his mother. Yolanda often asked Timothy why he didn't have a picture of her and he said that he saw her every day. Yolanda perched on the edge of the unforgiving chair and told Timothy her plans. He barely looked up from the totals of the tithes and offering and mumbled a short "uh-huh". Timothy scratched his head, irritated that the totals were down. The summer months took a toll on tithes and offerings, because vacations always took precedence over giving.

Yolanda hoped that wherever Timothy ate lunch, he would choke on a chicken bone, panicking as he drew in his last breath, wondering what life would be like on the other side, and which side he would see. She hoped he would feel the fear she felt every time he hit her; the fear of not knowing if you were going to live or die. She was sure Jesus wasn't happy with her right about now, but she couldn't help her feelings. Jesus said that you can't love Him and hate your brother, but Timothy made it so hard to love. Yolanda decided that she was not going to waste any more of her time thinking about Timothy. She didn't want to be in a bad mood when she arrived at Andre's home.

CHAPTER 8

Yolanda was nervous as she approached Andre's home, butterflies racing in the pit of her stomach. "Hi beautiful." Andre greeted her with a smile and fresh cut flowers after she pulled into the garage.

"Hi, Andre." They walked into his home and he seated her at the bar in the kitchen while he continued to prepare lunch. As she sipped on the iced tea that he poured, she stole glances at Andre beneath her long lashes.

"Is your tea sweet enough?"

"Yes, it's perfect." Yolanda couldn't help but notice Andre's muscles rippling beneath the black polo shirt as he stirred the risotto he was preparing. She shifted in her seat, her core becoming warm, thinking about being enveloped in Andre's strong arms.

After dining on rosemary baked chicken, risotto, and wilted greens, Yolanda and Andre retired to the living room to relax. Yolanda had become less anxious as the day progressed, and she felt comfortable when Andre draped his arm over her shoulder as they sat on his couch. She was amazed at what the human touch could do. His gentle hands offered her so much comfort and ease. Yolanda kicked her shoes off, and removed her scarf, forgetting about her battle scars. Andre's eyes widened in disbelief as he noticed the handprints on Yolanda's neck. He grabbed Yolanda around her waist, pulled her to him, and held her tight, almost unconsciously hurting her.

"Did Timothy do this?" he asked, still holding her and kissing the top of her head.

"Yes." Yolanda whimpered, wiping her eyes.

"Real men don't hit women. You know that you don't have to go back into that environment." Yolanda saw the veins pulsing in his neck." If you were my woman, you would be treated like a queen every day."

Yolanda felt the need to freshen up, and asked Andre if she could use his restroom.

"Follow me." Andre led Yolanda down the hall and into the master bedroom. Yolanda was pleasantly surprised at the layout of the room. The walls were chocolate with butter cream trim. Silk chocolate sheets and lots of cream and chocolate colored pillows graced the fabric enclosed king sized canopy bed. Flowing drapes that resembled rivers of cream on the windows rounded out the whole room. Yolanda wondered how a man could create such a romantic atmosphere, knowing the bedroom would be a haven for lovers.

"Who decorated your home? Everything is so beautiful. I love it."

"I did it all myself. My mother and grandmother always had the best of everything, top of the line. They were always up on new fashion trends and their homes were always immaculate." Andre smiled, grateful that Yolanda found his home warm and inviting. Andre walked into his closet and removed a thick, plush terry robe and tucked it under his arm.

"Come on." Andre walked into the bathroom. He walked over to the huge Jacuzzi and turned the brass faucets on and let the water flow into it.

"Yolanda, walk over to the vanity and choose a bath oil that you would like to soak in."

"You invite me to your home for the first time, and you expect me to take a relaxing soak? I don't think so, Andre. I am not that desperate." Yolanda was a bit miffed.

"Did I say you were desperate? Have I done anything to you that made you feel uncomfortable here today? We are both adults, and if you were not interested in me, you would not be here. I know this is unconventional, but I just want you to relax, and forget about your worries. Now, come choose an oil, but only if you feel comfortable doing so. There is absolutely no pressure."

As Yolanda looked into the vanity, she could hardly believe that a man would have so many oils, bubble baths and bath gels to choose from. "I'm sure that the many women you bed love the attention you pay to detail." Yolanda stated, as she picked up a bottle of Chamomile and Rose infused oil.

"You're right, I could bed as many women as I want, but I am waiting on someone special to make love to. And I will wait on you as long as I have to." Andre reached into one of the drawers and retrieved a barrette. He walked behind Yolanda and pulled her shoulder length hair into a loose bun and secured it with the barrette.

"How do you know so much about women?" Yolanda asked Andre as he poured a little of the oil in the flow of the water. He turned the faucets off and walked over to Yolanda. He placed her hands in his.

"I want to tell you everything about my life, the good, the bad, and the ugly. But right now, you need to relax. Just get undressed, hang your clothes on the hangers on the back of the door, soak all of your troubles away, and let them flow down the drain." He placed Yolanda's robe on the warming rack so that it would be warm when she got out.

Yolanda could not believe that she was soaking in a stranger's bath tub. Although there was no difference between being up close and personal with him and sitting in his tub, it was still out of character for her. Even though they talked on the phone, and went to dinner, she still really didn't know him. When she thought about it though, she really didn't care. A man was being nice to her, treating her like a lady, and showering her with attention, something she had craved for so long. Desperate times called for desperate measures.

Andre walked out of the bathroom and back out to the living room. He piped the sounds of smooth jazz throughout the house, hoping to soothe and calm Yolanda's frayed nerves. He lay down on the couch and closed his eyes, listening to the music.

His phone rang.

"Hello."

"What's up 'Dre?"

"What's up Warren?

"What's happening with you today?"

"Man I am chilling with the girl of my dreams. I have got to take my time with this one. I can't mess this up."

"What? 'Dre you can't be serious about this lady."

"Man you know me better than anyone else. You are my boy, and you have stood beside me through thick and thin. You know I have not even dated lately. I have been waiting for this one."

"Yes, and I also know that she is married. You better guard yourself man."

"Don't worry man. I'm taking it one day at a time. I am going to tell her all about my sordid past. I know that in order to have a meaningful relationship, honesty must be a priority, and even though we are far from being in one, I want to start off right. But, there is still one thing that I can never tell her."

"Man, be careful. I'm just saying. Love you, bro."

"Peace. Love you too man." Andre hung the phone up and closed his eyes once again, allowing the music to soothe away the wrinkle of worry that was trying to creep into his forehead.

Andre tapped on the bathroom door. "Are you alright in there?" He opened the door wide enough to squeeze his hand through, hoping she would tell him to come on in.

"Yes, I could stay in here forever. This is so relaxing."

"You better get out because I have never seen a good looking prune anywhere. A shriveled up woman has never done anything for me." Andre laughed, curiosity creeping up behind him, beckoning him to open the door a little more. Yolanda had never had an intimate encounter outside her marriage, but there was definitely a strong sexual connection that she could not deny. Yolanda decided that it was time to put out the fire that had raged relentlessly inside her and Andre would be the one to do it. Yolanda put the robe on, not tying the belt, and opened the door. Andre stood in the doorway, mesmerized. He pulled her to him, and kissed her softly, then hungrily, as he started to caress her body. Yolanda pulled away, suddenly self conscious about her inverted nipples.

"What's wrong?" Andre looked confused.

Yolanda embarrassingly told him.

"There is nothing wrong with inverted nipples, and they can temporarily correct during arousal."

"That's never happened before."

"That's because you've never been with the right man. Many women with your problem have them pierced, and the jewelry keeps them from becoming inverted again."

"How do you know so much about women?"

Without saying a word, Andre placed small kisses on her lips and caresses her lower back, that made her tingle all over. Yolanda began to moan with excitement and squeezed his biceps tightly, heightening her arousal. Andre proceeded to place tiny, sensual kisses on her entire abdomen, making his way to her flower. Then he kissed her hips, thighs, legs- even toes. Thinking that Andre was finished torturing her, Yolanda headed toward the bed to sit down, euphoric from the whole experience.

"Don't sit down. I'm not finished with you."

Andre pulled Yolanda from the bed and got down on the floor and nibbled all around her ankles and heel. He concentrated on the tiny circles that he made with his tongue on the back of her thighs. The small Z's he traced in her back with his tongue fueled the wildfire raging inside. He nibbled on her neck, sending her into an overflow that rocked her whole body. Yolanda collapsed, breathless on the floor, feeling light-headed, giddy, excited and nervous all at the same time. She would love to say that she felt guilty, and thought about what God was thinking, but she knew the truth. This man had awakened something inside her that was dead, and she liked living right about now.

"This day is all about you. I wanted to show you how deep my desire is for you, and that was just a small taste. Until next time." Andre pulled her up and pressed her body to his. Yolanda reluctantly backed away, and headed to the bathroom to shower, never wanting the good time to end. Andre followed her. "You know you never have to leave. Stay with me."

"As much as my body is telling me to stay, my mind says I must go home." Yolanda kissed Andre on the lips.

"When can I see you again?"

"How's next week sound?"

"What about tomorrow?"

Yolanda giggled. "As much as I would like that, it's not going to happen."

Yolanda thought about her encounter with Andre on the way home. How could something so wrong feel so right? Yolanda questioned how a saved, sanctified, Holy Ghost filled woman could be in a predicament like she was. How could she give in to deadly sins? She hoped that God would forgive her, but, she couldn't let Andre go just yet. She knows that if every woman told the truth, there would be a lot of First Ladies just like her; feeling lonely, second-fiddle, unloved, sex-starved, with husbands married to everyone and everything but them. They all needed an outlet, an escape. Yolanda was glad that she found hers.

CHAPTER 9

When Yolanda entered her house Timothy was sitting at the bar waiting for her. She was nervous inside, trying not to panic, wondering if he was aware of her indiscretion. His serious disposition did not help combat her fear.

"Is something wrong? You look so serious." Yolanda fidgeted with her keychain, hoping Timothy would not detect the nervousness in her voice. "Brian killed Tara". Yolanda saw his mouth moving, but was sure that he must have misspoken. Tears welled in Yolanda's eyes.

Showing no emotion, Timothy continued. "Tara wanted to leave." Timothy picked up his lemonade and drank long and slow. He fished out a couple of seeds that were in the glass and placed them on a napkin. "She told him that she was going to live with her parents, and Brian went to the bedroom, got a gun, and shot her point blank in the temple. I guess he just lost it." Timothy concluded, chugging the last of the lemonade and sucking on an ice cube.

Yolanda felt the room spinning and held onto the bar to steady herself, trying to calm the wave of nausea that had swept over her. She could no longer contain it and ran to the sink to release the foul truth that had filled her. Timothy still sat motionless in the chair. Yolanda wet a few paper towels and cleaned her face and mouth. She grabbed a Sprite from the fridge and took a few sips.

"You know that this is all your fault, don't you? You were supposed to be counseling them and helping them." He slammed his fists on the table and kicked the chair next to him. "What were you doing all this time in your sessions, and why didn't you report it? You know this publicity is bad for the church."

"Timothy, this is NOT my fault, and you know it!" Yolanda's face reddened and she moved toward Timothy, wanting to scratch his eyeballs out, anger seeping from every pore.

"The police had a restraining order against him because I reported the abuse, but Tara chose not to enforce it. When he raped her, I took her to the hospital's Rape Crisis Center. I also pleaded with her not to stop her counseling sessions, because I knew that Brian was a time bomb waiting to explode. She chose to ignore my please, and took Brian's empty promises. You don't care that Brian killed Tara! You only care about your stupid church and your image."

"What else is there, Yolanda? I have worked so hard to keep this church running smoothly, and I don't need any waves." Yolanda was crying hysterically at the loss of her friend and cringing at the sound of her husband's unsympathetic voice.

"What is wrong with you? Tara is dead, an unborn baby is dead, and you are worrying about your image. Are you crazy? Have you no feelings? Is there a heart in there?" Yolanda spewed, tapping Timothy on his chest.

"You are such a hypocrite, pretending to care about those people!" Yolanda turned to walk away, and a blow to her lower back sent her plummeting to the floor. Timothy stood over her, fists clenched.

"Don't you ever call me hypocrite again. You need to learn your place and watch your mouth. I rule this house!" Yolanda lay on the floor for what seemed like forever after he walked away. She was deathly afraid of Timothy, and knew that she should get up and run away, but a four letter word called fear kept her there. Yolanda finally stood up and limped to the cabinet. She popped two Tylenol PM tablets, and walked slowly upstairs, feeling her back spasm with every move.

Yolanda showered and lay down across the bed. Timothy walked in with a cup of green tea, and apologized for hurting her.

"You just need to watch your language. But, you can make it up to me by going to get me some Krispy Kreme doughnuts." Yolanda slowly climbed out of bed, dressed, and grabbed her purse, wondering how his heart could be so cold. Protesting would just be another fight, and at this point it wasn't worth it. She thought about how her life was beginning to mirror Tara's, and realized the end of the road was near.

When she returned home, Timothy was sitting in the den reading the Bible.

"I want to apologize again for earlier. Just make sure you remember what I said. So, let's just forget it happened, and start fresh. It's been a while since we've been intimate, so let's just start there."

"Timothy, I am sorry, but my back hurts. Do you think we can wait until tomorrow?" Yolanda never wanted Timothy to touch her again. One, she was tired of his abuse. Two, Andre made her feel like she had never felt before.

"Are you telling me no? The woman with the abnormal breasts, telling me no? You must be crazy. What did we just talk about earlier? Submission?"

Timothy walked over to Yolanda, shoved her down onto the couch. He hurriedly unbuckled and dropped his pants to the floor. Timothy pinned her head down with his elbow as he undressed her with his free hand. He entered her harshly, and had no regards for her as a person. The way Timothy ravaged her made her feel lower than a mange dog that need to be put out of its misery. Tears streamed down Yolanda's cheeks, but they could never match the dam that was about to break loose in her heart. Timothy finished his unthinkable act, pulled his pants up, and stood over Yolanda.

"Your weak sobs don't move me. I am so sick of you whining and crying all the time. You should be glad somebody wants to sleep with your fat butt. I've told you a hundred times, nobody wants you, not even me. Hurry up, get showered and dressed. Tara's family is expecting us."

Yolanda pulled her pants up and sat on the couch, whimpering. She realized that she had to do something to change the dreadful situation she was in, but couldn't muster up the courage. She wanted to call the police, her parents; someone had to know she needed help..... *Why isn't anyone helping me?*

As soon as they pulled up to Tara's house, Yolanda noticed how nice and well-kept the yard was. The small brick ranch was accentuated by a plethora of shrubs and flowers in various stages of bloom. As they walked into the house they were greeted by Tara's mother. Her already round face was swollen even more from the endless tears that she had shed. Yolanda hugged Tara's mother for what seemed an eternity, hoping that she could feel how much she cared about Tara.

"We are so sorry, Mrs. Johnson. If there is anything that you need, please let us know. Tara was one of the most caring people that I've ever met in my life. She didn't deserve to die... not like this...." Yolanda felt the hot tears burning as they fell from her eyes. "

I know sweetie. I know that you loved Tara. You gave her everything she needed to escape Brian's torment. In the end, she made the right choice. But, it was just a little too late....." Mrs. Johnson wiped her eyes again, making them even redder than before.

After consoling Tara's family, Timothy and Yolanda left. The day had been long, and Yolanda was emotionally, mentally, and physically drained. If she were to write a book about her life, no one would believe her. It was too crazy, too unbelievable to be true. Quiet consumed the car during the drive home. Yolanda had too many thoughts crowding her mind at the same time. She thought about Andre. He made her feel alive. For the first time in years, she felt something inside her move. Was it her heart beating again; coming back to life? Her thoughts drifted to Timothy. Yolanda was worn-out from the abuse, and realized that if she didn't start to make plans to escape her end would be just like Tara's. Her stomach churned as her mind revisited Timothy raping her earlier. She understood that it was a power move, another means to control her. He would stoop to the lowest depths of the earth, to try and put her in the hell he would surely burn in. Then she thought about Tara, the poor misguided soul; wanting to believe against all odds that fairy tales and dreams come true. Yolanda thought about the pain, anger and resentment Tara's parents must have been going through. She felt like strangling Brian herself, and could only imagine how they felt.

When they arrived home, Yolanda went straight to the bedroom, put her pajamas on and went to bed. She prayed that Timothy would let her rest, and asked God to help her not breathe too loud.

CHAPTER 10

The next few days were a blur to Yolanda. She had to retrieve the leftover Lortab from her wisdom tooth extraction out of the medicine cabinet, just to be able to function. The physical toll on her body from Timothy's brutality, plus the emotional toll of Tara's death, had taken her over the edge.

It was two o'clock on a Thursday afternoon and Yolanda scrambled to get dressed for Tara's funeral. She carefully pulled up her last set of thigh-highs, hoping she wouldn't ruin them like she had the first pair. Living with Timothy always made her think ahead. She normally purchased two of everything breakable, tear-able, or rippable—just in case. The consequences of not planning were always detrimental to her health. After dressing, Yolanda gave herself the once over in the mirror, and hoped that Timothy would approve.

As Yolanda walked down the aisle of BrightStar towards Tara's casket, she was sickened and angry listening to Timothy drone on about how wonderful Tara was. Yolanda knew that he could have cared less about Tara being dead. Everything he was saying was just a front, to make people think that he had feelings. But, she lived with the man behind the mask. Yolanda could hardly look at Tara's swollen, misshapen face. Tara's parents insisted on having an open casket so that other victims of abuse could see the final straw; which was death. Yolanda noticed the small brown teddy bear nestled in her arms. Her white frilly gown made her look like an angel. She looked like she was finally at peace.

Yolanda sat on the seat with the family, trying not to cry out loud as the choir soothed them with an old hymn. Timothy would certainly punish her for making a scene. She thought about something else to take her mind off Tara. Yolanda wondered if she would ever become a mother. She was so tired of Timothy telling her that if she would just relax, and stop being so uptight, she could get pregnant. He also loved to tell her that God had shut up her womb, and until she became a submissive wife, she would never get pregnant. Yolanda wished that she had the nerve to tell him that she never wanted to have his child anyway. He was a walking time bomb, ready to explode at any minute. If everyone knew that Yolanda herself was a contender in the domestic violence arena, the whole church would be sent reeling.

After the funeral, Tara's parents thanked Yolanda for the years she spent counseling her.

"First Lady, we know that you did all you could for Tara. We know that you tried to steer her away from Brian, and we are grateful. Still, the pain won't go away." Tara's mother sobbed, placing her head on Yolanda's shoulder. Yolanda held her tight, hoping that a hug would somehow heal the pain, but accepting that it couldn't.

"Mrs. Johnson, I am so sorry." Tara's mother released Yolanda from the death grip, and kissed her on the cheek. Yolanda noticed that her eyes were still red and puffy, wounded from unspeakable despair. Yolanda turned and walked away, unable to take any more of the sadness. After the funeral she greeted as many members as she could, her eyes constantly filled with water, her heart aching.

Yolanda watched Timothy devour his food as they sat at the Pastor's table with Tara's parents and siblings. As everyone else picked at their food, Timothy was eating like he was at a family reunion. Yolanda was embarrassed, and tried not to look at him. Knowing that she could not correct him in front of everyone, she ignored him.

"Don't you all think Sister Kay makes the best macaroni and cheese and fried chicken?" Timothy was smiling and laughing, like they hadn't just put Tara in the ground. A few of the pastor's minstrels chimed in, agreeing. Yolanda was sickened by their behavior and looked forward to Timothy finishing his meal, so that she could get home and go to bed. The Lortab was kicking in, and sleep beckoned her.

When Yolanda arrived home, she was drained and decided to take a bubble bath. She marveled at how her life has gone from victim's advocate to victim. The subject was too deep for her to dwell on, and her thoughts drifted to Andre. She couldn't wait to see him. Her body longed for his touch. Yolanda had already peeked at Timothy's schedule, and he would be in a men's conference all day on Saturday. Yolanda found it ironic that she was afraid of her husband finding out about Andre, like God didn't know. She rationalized since she was being abused, God would overlook her adulterous relationship with Andre. It certainly wasn't true, but like millions of other Christians, she didn't care at the moment. She would freely give in to all her desires, and deal with the consequences later.

Friday rolled around, and Yolanda decided to go to the office, just to catch up on paperwork. Her secretary had cancelled all of her sessions as soon as she found out about Tara's death. Yolanda made a mental note to write her a thank you note. She pulled Tara's thick file and began to read the details of her first session. Tara used to come alone for quite some time, until she finally convinced Brian to join her. A fresh crop of tears to came to Yolanda's eyes as she looked back over the folder at Tara's naivety, and she decided that she would finish some other tasks. She put the file back into the drawer and closed it.

After Yolanda finished with the paperwork, she called Andre to see if their plans for the weekend were still on. She desperately needed a distraction.

"Hello, Yolanda." Andre answered as he lowered the dumbbell to the floor. His home gym came in handy for maintaining his rock hard body.

"Hello, yourself." Yolanda purred, feeling like an elementary school girl with a serious crush.

"I hope you're not calling to cancel tomorrow, because the anticipation is killing me. I just want to hold you in my arms and smell your sweetness." Yolanda felt her body relaxing as she listened to Andre's voice.

"I'll be there with bells on. What time should I arrive?"

"As soon as you can. I am an early riser so let's say six a.m.? I'll make you breakfast." Yolanda laughed because they both knew that she would not be able to get out of the house that soon.

"I'll be there at nine. The conference starts at eight o'clock and Timothy will be out of the house at seven, getting prepared. And I'll come hungry. See ya then." Yolanda placed her Blackberry on the desk, leaned back in her chair and closed her eyes. She couldn't wait to see Andre. A deep smile crossed her face as she thought about the satisfaction that he brought her. In order to make it through the rest of the day, she had to stop thinking about Andre, or the excitement would overtake her.

Later on that evening, Yolanda made a black and bleu salad for dinner. It wasn't too heavy for the hot summer heat, and was easy to prepare. A sirloin steak cooked and sliced, romaine lettuce, fresh veggies and bleu cheese dressing and dinner was ready. A thick slice of garlic bread and a glass of iced tea topped off the meal. Yolanda started making the salad on her own after repeatedly spending ten dollars at O'Charleys for a salad and drink.

Timothy came in and without so much as a hello, and followed his normal routine of showering. Yolanda didn't care what he did anymore. Timothy's abusive behavior toward her had made her heart for him a plate of steel. Timothy sat down at the table and they ate in silence until he spoke.

"Yolanda, I am sorry about what happened. *Which time?* Yolanda wondered to herself. She knew not to say anything aloud to get him riled.

"But, I can't say that it won't happen again. Everything that happens from now on is dependent on you. All you have to do is submit. My grandfather had this dog, and this dog had a bad habit of trying to bite him. Every time that dog snapped at him, he would crack his ribs with a broom." Timothy took a huge bite of salad and Yolanda was mesmerized at the remnants of salad dressing in the corners of his mouth as he spoke. "I remember thinking that he was so cruel for beating the dog like that. I asked him why he hit him so hard. He said that everyone says "you can't teach old dog new tricks", but he begged to differ. 'You just watch and see, after this dog has had enough beatings, he'll never snap at me again.' "I didn't understand it then, but now I do." Timothy said, as he inhaled another mouthful of salad.

Yolanda wanted to bash his head in after her comparison to a dog. How he could even try to rationalize that statement made her almost hate him. She knew that it was over between her and Timothy, whether he knew it or not. Yolanda couldn't say that she knew everything about God, but she knew he would not want her to stay in an abusive relationship. How Timothy had gotten so distracted from the real meaning of ministry had her bewildered. All Timothy was concerned about was the church's image, how much the church was growing, and how much money came in. Forget about the people who sacrificed time and money weekly to keep the church running. Not to mention those who thought Timothy was the best thing that ever happened to them. They almost worshipped the ground he walked on and thought he could do no wrong. Yolanda didn't worry though, because the Bible said what was done in darkness, would come to the light, and that didn't exclude her either.

After Yolanda cleaned the kitchen, she prepared for bed. Timothy's insane ramblings had left her exhausted. Yolanda showered, read a few passages of scripture, and put on her satin bonnet to keep her hair tight. Her mouth began to water, as if she had tasted something foul. He always wanted to be intimate with her days later after raping her. Yolanda felt it was his sick, twisted way of offering an apology after raping her. She struggled to hold the vomit that threatened to escape her throat.

"Timothy." Yolanda chose her words very carefully. "I think that salad upset my stomach. Could we wait until tomorrow?" Timothy turned over and faced the wall and was soon asleep. Yolanda was thankful that he accepted her explanation. Having sex with Timothy had become a thing of the past.

CHAPTER 11

Yolanda rose early and cooked a full breakfast for Timothy with a smile. The grits, scrambled eggs, country ham with red eye gravy, toast and fresh cantaloupe was enough to feed an army. She was only thinking of Andre. The ground up Senekot laxative in Timothy's eggs also kept the smile on her face. She had been thinking long and hard about the physical pain and emotional suffering that he put her through, and she decided to get even, in her own way.

Just imagining Timothy running from the pulpit to the restroom was enough to almost make Yolanda laugh out loud. He would never guess the culprit because the church would be preparing breakfast also, and Timothy would have to eat a little something just to keep the peace among the church ladies. Yolanda made sure she emptied the laxatives from the container and threw the package in the garbage outside the grocery store. She then put the laxatives in a snack-sized baggie and placed them in her purse and ground them the days before in her coffee grinder. She always kept an abundance of spices so Timothy would have never known what it was anyway.

Timothy entered the kitchen without as much as a good morning, and grabbed a plate from the cabinet. He prepared his plate, loading it down with everything Yolanda had cooked, and sat at the table. He said a short grace and dove in. Timothy wolfed down his food, and got up and left, not even bothering to clear his plate from the table.

Yolanda prepared a small bowl of grits and a piece of toast for herself. She didn't want to make Timothy suspicious. Andre said to come hungry, with only the clothes on her back and a purse. Even though Yolanda had purchased some nice lingerie, Andre insisted that he had everything taken care of. Yolanda nibbled on the toast and thought about her life, and accepted that it was over between her and Timothy. And try as she might, Yolanda still could not believe that Timothy was hitting her. It's almost as if she was outside looking in. Recognizing that she was about to commit adultery, she persuaded herself that God would forgive her, because she was a battered wife, and He was a God of love and peace.

Timothy walked over and kissed the top of Yolanda's head before he headed out. The firm squeeze on her shoulder was a subtle hint that he was in control. "I will be home by seven. What are your plans for the day?" "I will probably do some shopping for some new church clothes, find a new chair for my office, and visit my parents." Yolanda held her breath, waiting for his answer. She had to make up something to get away, knowing he wouldn't let her venture out alone too much. "Since you haven't seen your parent's in a while, I will let you visit." Timothy tried to remember the last time he had spoken with Yolanda's parents. Never would still be too soon in his book.

Yolanda arrived at Andre's home a little after nine-thirty a.m. Andre waited as Yolanda pulled her car inside the garage. He hoped that Yolanda would not feel his rapid heartbeat when she got close to him. The cream-colored silk blouse and mocha crop pants hugged every curve of her figure. The mocha stiletto heels further accentuated her femininity and every step she took toward him almost made him salivate. Yolanda's shoulder length hair was pulled into a neat chignon, and her million-dollar smile was the clincher. The smile was it. It said that she wanted to be there, and that's all Andre needed to know. Yolanda fell into his arms and gave him a long hug. Andre reciprocated, feeling that he had never felt such a connection with a woman before, and he didn't want to lose it. "Wow, you look great today, Yolanda. Girl, I could sop you up with a biscuit." Andre laughed and finally released her from his death grip. He lightly brushed his lips against hers, sending an instant message to his brain that he was aroused. "Let's go and eat before I get crazy out here." Andre scooped Yolanda up into his arms and walked inside.

Andre carried Yolanda down the hall and into the large master bathroom. He put her down and slowly removed every stitch of her clothing. Yolanda was calm, not even worrying about her body's imperfections. Andre loved the feel of the silk mocha bra and panty set in his hand, and he placed it on the vanity with her other clothing. "The clothes hangers will have to wait." Andre wrapped Yolanda's naked body in a warm robe and secured it with a belt and led her to the sink. He placed her hands into the large hand-blown glass basin and wooden stand that was in the corner of the bathroom. The bowl was beautiful; its vibrant colors reminded her of a school of tropical fish, and she realized that whoever made the bowl put a piece of their soul into it. Andre glued himself to her, and gently washed each of her fingers. He placed her palms face up over the bowl and poured warm water from a matching glass pitcher directly into the center of each palm. Yolanda didn't even try to mask the ecstasy that was building inside like a jet engine. She closed her eyes and let out a small sigh.

Andre carried Yolanda into the kitchen and placed her on the island barstool next to his workstation. He removed crispy bacon and sautéed vegetables from the oven warmer and placed them on top of the stove. The smell of peppery bacon and onions, mushrooms, red and green bell peppers wafted through the air. Yolanda noticed that he used Wisconsin mild white cheddar instead of regular cheddar. Andre made Yolanda a mimosa, and she sipped it slowly, feeling the champagne warm her already heated insides more. She crossed her legs allowing the robe to part, exposing her thigh. Andre stopped cooking and nestled his head in her lap and kissed her thighs. "If you don't stop distracting me, there will be no breakfast." Andre willed himself away from Yolanda and resumed cooking. Yolanda laughed out loud and threw her head back, allowing Andre to gaze into her open mouth. "I'm going to remember this torture later." Yolanda watched as Andre meticulously prepared the quiche and placed it into the oven. Her insides began to rumble and she didn't know if it was hungry for food, or hungry for love. Andre poured himself a mimosa and positioned himself in front of Yolanda, running his fingers up her exposed thighs. "What can we do for the next twenty minutes while breakfast is cooking?" Andre slid his tongue into her mouth. Yolanda let her mouth talk for her as she hungrily received Andre's deep kisses.

The beep of the oven jarred them both out of the sensual zone that they were enveloped in. They both reclaimed their breathing and Andre walked over to the stove, removed the quiche and placed it on a cooling rack. "Ten more minutes and we are ready to eat." Andre smiled and looked at Yolanda, realizing that this was going to be one of the best days of his life. He refreshed the mimosas and asked Yolanda to have a seat in the dining room. Yolanda walked into the dining room and was surprised by the candles and china that met her glance. She had heard of candlelight dinners, but never a candlelight breakfast. Andre seated her at the table and walked back to the kitchen to get the quiche. Yolanda marveled at Andre's creativity and romantic inclinations as she sipped her mimosa.

After a delectably mouth-watering breakfast, Andre and Yolanda retired to the Jacuzzi, au natural. Yolanda laid her head on Andre's chest as he began to massage her inner thighs with his thumbs. The slow, deliberate circles made Yolanda moan with pleasure. He planted soft kisses on her neck. Yolanda felt as if her body is on fire. She was almost afraid, because she had never experienced passion on a level like this before. She had never known the fiery pangs that throbbed inside her existed. Even though she and Timothy were intimate during their happier days, Yolanda always remembered thinking that something was missing. She now knew what it was. Andre placed light kisses on her back. Yolanda tried to maneuver one of Andre's hands, but he resisted. "There's no rush, we have all day."

Andre stood up, and grabbed the robes and stepped out of the Jacuzzi, leaving Yolanda speechless. Andre was definitely the total package that women fantasized about. The water dripping from the black Adonis made her gasp. He wrapped a robe around himself and then wrapped one around Yolanda as she stepped out. "I have a present for you." Andre led Yolanda to the bedroom. He walked to the closet and pulled out a large black bag with a big red bow. "I hope you like it." Yolanda smiled and pulled the bow off the bag, looking inside. A nice black negligee by Nina Ricci with a scoop neck and low cut back was the first item to come out of the bag. Next, was a bottle of Chanel No. 5 perfume and velvet body cream. The last item she removed from the bag was a journey diamond necklace. The necklace had to be worth a small fortune. "Andre, you know that I cannot accept this. This is beautiful, but I just can't accept it. What would Timothy say if he saw me wearing this necklace?" Andre placed his index finger on Yolanda's lips, and draped the necklace around her neck and fastened it. "Just wear it for now. Could you humor me for the moment? I don't want this moment to be a fling. I want this to be a step towards you being my wife. I want nothing more than to wake up to your lovely face every morning. And, the added plus of this banging body doesn't hurt either." Andre smiled as he lightly squeezed her cheeks. The smile disappeared and Andre seemed so serious that it shook Yolanda a little. "You will be my wife. I have waited and prayed for someone just like you. I know God doesn't make mistakes, and we are together for a reason. I know that you feel it too, or you wouldn't be here. This is more that just a fling, or lust, or sex, this is a new beginning for both of us, and it's perfect in every way."

Andre picked Yolanda up and carried her to the bed, and lay down beside her. He rubbed her entire body in the velvet body cream, taking his time, enjoying every moment. He looked into her eyes for the longest time, looking deep into her soul. Yolanda returned the gaze, longing for the love that filled his eyes. Andre kissed her for an eternity, savoring every morsel of moisture that escaped from her lips. He touched her so gently, sending messages of intense pleasure to her brain. Andre spent hours making love to Yolanda, not leaving one area of her body untouched. Yolanda felt her insides open up like never before, the sensation was strange but pleasurable at the same time. Yolanda now understood what true passion was, and trembled as the new sensations ripped through her body. Breathless, they kissed one another as they collapsed into one another's arms. Andre pulled Yolanda on top of him and held her tightly. "I really like you Yolanda. I don't want this to end." "I must say, I like you too, Mr. Hunter." Yolanda kissed Andre and they both drifted off to a deep sleep.

Andre and Yolanda awoke to the doorbell's constant ringing, then to loud knocks on the front door. Andre dressed hurriedly and ran to the bathroom to wash his face and swish his mouth with mouthwash. He jogged down the hallway to the foyer to see what could be so urgent. Andre almost stumbled when he looked through the sidelights to see Vicki standing at his door. His head began to spin, wondering why Vicki was outside his home, how she found him again, and how he would explain to Yolanda why she was there. Anger crept up on him and he felt like he could choke the living hell out of Vicki. He had just poured out his heart to Yolanda, and now, if she saw Vicki, she would never believe anything he said. Andre opened the door, whispering. "What the hell are you doing here, Vicki?"

"Is that any way to talk to your future wife? Shouldn't you be greeting me with a kiss?" Vicki tried to saunter into the house. Andre blocked her way.

"Vicki, you are not coming into my home. You are not welcome here, and never will be. What we had is in the past, and I ain't trying to resurrect nothing that's dead. So, turn around and be on your way. If you come back around here, I will take out a restraining order on you." Vicki's eyes became dark and cynical. She slapped Andre as hard as she could and begins screaming obscenities at him. Andre sensed that Yolanda would soon be behind him and feels his fists clenching. He had to pray not to hit Vicki, and that the rage in him would die. Now, instead of being able to tell Yolanda about his past in a calm manner, it all would come out like a fireworks show on the Fourth of July.

Vicki stops yelling as her eyes adjusted to the woman coming toward her. "Yolanda? What are you doing here?" An inquisitive look crossed Vicki's face. "My, my, my... wouldn't Timothy love to be a fly on the wall. What's going on Yolanda?" Vicki smiled, enjoying her supposed opportunity to hurt Yolanda once again.

"The question is, Vicki, why are you here? You don't need to know anything about my life anymore, so don't even ask or act like you are concerned. You are nothing but a slut and that's all you will ever be, so why don't you just leave!" Yolanda found herself trembling with fury, and she wanted to scratch Vicki's eyes out. How could she keep interfering in her life? First, she had to interfere with her marriage to Timothy, now Andre. How could one woman keep punishing her, reminding her that she could take her man?

"I am sure that your husband doesn't know that you are here, Yolanda. Maybe I will stop by and say hello, and tell him that you are at another man's house letting him rock your world! Andre is the best, and from what I can remember, he sure knows how to make a girl feel good." Vicki said as she seductively stroked his cheek.

Yolanda lunged forward and grabbed Vicki by the collar. She was so close to her face that she fogged the shades that Vicki was wearing with her hot breath. "You have threatened me for the last time. I thought you were my friend, but you were nothing but a two-bit tramp trying to get your claws into my husband. Now, you want to insert your claws into Andre." Vicki tried to break away from Yolanda, but her concrete grip tightened and she pulled Vicki even closer. "You will not say anything to Timothy about me being here today. You will not come back to this house. If you do, you will write your death sentence. Today has been the best day of my life, and the worst day of my life. I have gained everything I have every desired, and lost it just now. So, I have nothing to lose. If you tell Timothy, I will kill you. Don't try me." Yolanda released Vicki and turned and walked back down the hallway, as if nothing ever happened.

Vicki stood in the doorway, visibly shaken, the color gone from her face. She was as street as street could be, but for some reason, she was afraid of Yolanda. But deep down, she knew why she was afraid. Yolanda was serious, and she meant business. Vicki accepted that she had wounded her for the last time, because Yolanda felt as if she had nothing else to lose. Vicki could not believe that the mild mannered Pastor's wife had a dark side. Vicki could literally smell the stench of death on Yolanda's breath as she spoke, and she was not going to stay around long enough to see if she would be true to her word. Vicki straightened out the collar of her blouse and adjusted her miniskirt, hands still trembling, and walked away.

Andre closed the door and took a deep breath. He didn't even know where to begin trying to explain to Yolanda about his relationship with Vicki. The hard part would be getting her to open up again. Andre prayed that Yolanda will be receptive to him and that they would be able to work through everything that had just transpired.

Andre walked into the bedroom. Yolanda had already taken a quick shower and was putting on her clothes. She didn't even look up at him and Andre could feel the fierce anger exuding from her pores. "Yolanda, give me a chance to explain." Yolanda kept moving quickly about the room, packing her belongings, not even giving Andre the time of day. As far as she was concerned, it was over. Nothing mattered to her anymore. Maybe God was angry with her for committing adultery and it was his cruel joke to let her experience true passion just once, before yanking it all away. Yolanda acknowledged deep down that she couldn't blame God. What she did was wrong, and sometimes God has to let us make our own mistakes and learn from them. Yolanda realized that if Andre knew Vicki, he had to know her all along, from the church commercials, and she felt set up. She couldn't figure out what kind of scam they were trying to pull, but she would find out. She wanted to, but surmised that it would not be wise, to ask Timothy how Andre and Vicki were connected. Timothy would want to know how she knew Andre, and that was a can of worms not worth opening. She was not even worried about Vicki talking to Timothy about her affair with Andre, because

Vicki was an opportunist, and she would not risk her money from Timothy getting cut off. Yolanda was even angrier, thinking about how Vicki was spending her auntie's money.

"Yolanda." Andre stood in front of her and rested his hands on her waist. The hard slap from Yolanda told him that she would not be listening to anything he had to say. "Yolanda, Vicki is a part of my past, and I had no idea she was coming here today. I haven't seen her in years. You have to believe me. We need to sit down and talk about this now. Let's just get everything out in the open and I will tell you everything about me and my past."

"I don't want to know anything about you or your past. You played me and you won. Now you and Vicki can go to hell." Yolanda yanked the necklace off her neck and threw it at Andre. "I'm going home to my husband, where I should have been in the first place. I should have never fallen for your smooth lines and your smile. Don't ever call me again. Forget that you ever knew me."

Yolanda grabbed her belongings and ran past Andre out to the garage. Andre knew that trying to reason with her would not help, so he let the garage door up for her. Yolanda got into her car, and slammed the door. She put the car in reverse and sped out of the garage and driveway, not even looking back. She hoped that Andre didn't think his fake countenance was going to get to her. Yolanda could have slapped herself silly for telling him that she liked him. She played right into his little web of deceit, and became his prey.

As she drove home, she decided that she would fast and pray, and get back into right fellowship with God. Yolanda found the migraine medicine in her purse and swallowed three of them dry. Timothy would be coming home late tonight and she dreaded hearing all about the conference. She decided that she would take a long bath, dry her tears, and face the reality of her life as a pastor's wife. An abused woman hidden from the world; no name, no identity, forever The Sunday Morning Wife. A woman who would have to endure being second fiddle and being physically abused for the rest of her life.

CHAPTER 12

Andre stood in the garage, staring at the empty space where Yolanda's car was parked. He too, felt like God had played a cruel joke, and was now laughing at the outcome. He returned to the bedroom and removed the three-carat platinum diamond from his top drawer. He would never get the chance to place the ring on her finger. Andre threw the box against the wall and used every obscenity that he remembered. He cursed as he threw everything in sight, angry that he has lost his chance on a relationship with a decent woman. He continued to curse until he didn't have any breath left. "God, how can you do this to me? I give up a life of crime, sex and everything else to serve you. You promised me long life and prosperity, and you even had the preacher say I would find a wife. Now, I find her and you take her away from me. Why should I live for you? You have taken away the very thing that I even live for? I thought that I would find peace and joy in you. Now, you have turned my life upside down, and I have only sorrow and despair. Why are you doing this to me? Timothy has been cheating on her for years with Vicki! I could make her a good husband!" Andre sat on the bed, too weary and angry to give the situation any more thought, and went to sleep.

Yolanda woke up and stared at the clock. It was seven o'clock in the morning and Timothy wasn't even home. She picked up the phone and dialed his cell phone. "Yolanda, I knew you would be calling soon." "Timothy, where are you?" Yolanda rose from the bed and looked in the mirror at her bloodshot eyes. "I left you a message around eight, but I guess you were out shopping and didn't bother to listen. What time did you get home yesterday?" "About five thirty. I must have been in the bath when you called. All the shopping wore me out so I went to bed early, and thought you would wake me when you came home." Yolanda was so glad that Timothy wasn't home to gauge her lies, because her palms were sweaty and she was fidgety. He would definitely know that she was lying if he saw her, and she wasn't in the mood for a beating. The way she was feeling today though, Timothy might be in for a surprise if he tried anything. She was so tired, so angry, and looking for any excuse to release her pent up frustration. "Timothy, I am not going to make it to church today. I have a migraine." Yolanda waited for the barrage of insults to start, but surprisingly, there were none. As strange as it was, Yolanda welcomed the change, thinking that maybe her marriage to Timothy was salvageable after all. "You sure are in a good mood, Timothy. Apostle Greene must have given you something in the conference that touched you deep down."

"Yolanda, I can't begin to tell you how clear everything is now. I am so excited about what God is doing. Listen, I've got to go get ready. I am going to shower and change here at the church. I guess the change of clothes you insisted I keep here will come in handy after all. See ya later."

Yolanda couldn't put her finger on it, but Timothy sounded almost giddy. What could Apostle Greene have told him that made him so happy? Yolanda didn't care. If it was going to keep Timothy smiling, it had to be good.

Yolanda showered and combed her hair into a chignon. She put on her silk robe and went into her walk-in closet. This was her altar, her secret closet, and it had been a while since she visited it- to pray anyway. She anointed herself with oil and got down on her knees. She thought that she had found true happiness with Andre, but realized that she was searching for love in all the wrong places. She had committed adultery, and now she had a soul tie with Andre. Only God could help her now. Yolanda repented and prayed like never before. She wept and cried out before the Lord, reminding Him who He was, and what He could do. She spoke His Word back to Him, and asked for forgiveness of her sins. Yolanda stayed in the closet for over an hour repenting, praying and rejoicing in the Lord, who was now her only strength. When she came out, she felt renewed and as light as a feather. All of her worries and cares were left there on the altar.

Yolanda ate oatmeal and drank a cup of coffee for breakfast. After eating, she curled up on the couch to read the Bible, but ended up falling asleep.

"Yolanda, wake up." Yolanda woke up wide-eyed and looked at Timothy. "What's wrong with you?"

"Nothing, you just startled me, that's all. What time is it?"

"It is three-fifteen in the afternoon."

"Why are you home so late?"

"Apostle Greene came to church and I had some business to tie up after services."

"So, when am I going to meet this man that's taking all my auntie's money?" Timothy's dark countenance told Yolanda that she had made a mistake. The slap to her face showed her. Yolanda sat on the couch, looking straight ahead, not blinking. She could not believe that she had prayed to God to help her love this man in spite of all he had done to her. He told her she was second fiddle to the church. He beat her unmercifully. He told her that she would never be able to carry his child. Yet, she asked for forgiveness and asked God to help her be a submissive wife. Now, hours later, her husband had slapped the taste out of her mouth. Yolanda realized something very important right then and there. Although she understood that God heard her prayer to touch Timothy and have him stop hitting her, because of the free will that God gives, he could only touch Timothy's heart, convicting him. It was totally up to Timothy whether or not he would accept God's conviction. Yolanda concluded that Timothy had no intention of changing. She slowly rose from the couch and went upstairs to the bedroom. Tomorrow would be a new day.

CHAPTER 13

Yolanda stuffed the rest of the McGriddle into her mouth. She had hit rock bottom, and food was her only comfort. She had to finish it before she walked inside the church. There was no way she could let Timothy find out she was eating calorie and fat-laden food. The *diet Coke should cancel out some of the calories...* Yolanda chugged the last of the drink and made her way into her office after exchanging pleasantries with her secretary. She looked over her appointment schedule and waited for her first appointment.

Yolanda finished her first three sessions and was happy that they all went amazingly smooth. She took a long swig of her bottled water and got up to use the restroom. Just as she's about to close the door, Amy walked in. "Well, hello there you!" Yolanda walked over to hug Amy. "I will be right out. Make yourself comfy."

When Yolanda returned from the restroom, Amy was sitting and looking out the window. "So, what's going on with you Amy?" Yolanda sat at her desk and listened intently as Amy relayed her concerns. Even though she had agreed to allow Amy to schedule a three-month follow-up after she completed the questionnaire, Yolanda sensed that something was bothering her because she was not due for her appointment. "My boyfriend J.R. is pressuring me to have sex, and I am just not ready." "Amy, don't sound so apologetic. Sex is a very sacred experience that God instituted for married couples and that you should not feel pressured into doing anything that you don't want to do." Yolanda wondered if Amy can see the large red "A" on her chest as she expounded on premarital sex and the dangers of it.

After their session was over, the friendly chitchat began. Yolanda understood that she was breaking all of the rules by establishing a relationship with a client, but she felt sorry for Amy and really enjoyed being a mentor to her. Amy was even taking some college courses and planned to major in Psychology.

"How is that guy doing we met at the mall? Maybe you could hook me up with him?" Yolanda almost choked on the bottled water that she was sipping.

"Amy, Mr. Hunter is too old for you first of all. Secondly, you cannot jump from one relationship where you are experiencing difficulty. And thirdly, you know nothing about Mr. Hunter."

"Mr s. Yolanda, don't get all upset about it! You act like I'm trying to take your man!" Yolanda tried to calm herself and hoped she can smooth out the wrinkles that she had put in the sheet of deception she was weaving.

"Amy, I am sorry if I came across too strong, but I just don't want to see you hurt, that's all. Please accept my apology if I offended you."

"Don't sweat it Mrs. Yolanda, everything is cool. I am going to go talk to J.R. and tell him I am not ready for a sexual relationship, and if he jets, he jets. Thanks for making time for me."

"I will always have time for you Amy. Don't ever forget that."

Amy left the office and Yolanda sat at her desk, sighing loudly. She was both nervous and irritated at the same time. Nervous because she wondered how much Amy read into her adulterous relationship with Andre, and irritated because Andre had broken her heart in record time. Yolanda understood that she sinned willingly by sleeping with Andre, and she knew God had forgiven her, but why could she not stop thinking about him? She fought the urge every day to pick up the phone and call him. She knew his number by heart, even though his number was on speed dial. Yolanda pressed the speed dial key and let the phone ring once. She hurriedly hung the phone up and grabbed her purse and left. Anger surged through her veins as she thought about how Andre had played her. Fresh pain pierced her heart as she remembered how he had broken it. Even though six weeks, two days, and two and a half hours had gone by, longing penetrated her whenever she reminisced about how he made love to her.

There was only one way to end everything once and for all; Andre would receive a surprise visit. Even though it was only twelve thirty, her schedule was clear for the rest of the day. Yolanda didn't even know if Andre would be home. If he was there, Vicki would probably be there too, but Yolanda didn't care. She had to put all of the cards on the table and get Andre out of her system, so that she could get on with her life.

Yolanda drove up to Andre's home and grabbed her straw hat with the wide brim that she always kept in the car. The summer sun was really angry today, and mimicked her mood. Yolanda went to the front door and rang the doorbell. Andre opened the door.

"Yolanda, I am so glad you're here. I saw your number on the caller I.D. I really need to talk to you." Andre couldn't figure out if he felt or saw the slap first. He rubbed his jaw where her fingerprints probably still were.

"Whatever it takes for you to release your anger, go ahead and get it out. Then we can sit down and talk like sensible adults." Andre didn't realize he was about to unleash the dragon when he told Yolanda that. Yolanda hit him with a barrage of kicks, punches and slaps, curses and bites. Andre shielded himself as best as he could and tried to restrain Yolanda while making sure he didn't hurt her. Andre never knew that the docile, kind Yolanda could have such a volatile side.

"I hate you Andre and I hate all of the drama that you have brought into my life. You have caused me nothing but pain. A low-down dirty dog wouldn't treat me the way you have. You told me you loved me, got me in bed, and Vicki just happens to drop in on the same day. Do you think that I am a fool? I may be a Pastor's wife, a goody two-shoes church girl, but I am not stupid. You got what you wanted, and I hope that you are happy. You will not ever have to worry about seeing me again. I just wanted to let you know how much you disgust me." Yolanda lunged at Andre once again and he sidestepped her and caught her from behind. Andre wrapped his arms tightly around Yolanda and squeezed her until he thought he was going to suffocate her. Yolanda kicked and squirmed in his arms.

"Let me go! Let me go! I hate you Andre! I hate everything about you!" Yolanda realized she sounded like a child, but could care less, and Andre held her tighter. Yolanda kicked and screamed some more until she couldn't even muster enough energy to swat a fly. She fell limp in Andre's arms and he carried her to the couch and lay her down. He handed her a box of Kleenex and went to the closet and retrieved a blanket and pillow. He covered her with the blanket and placed the pillow under her head, knowing not to get to close. Andre went to the kitchen and made her a cup of green tea with a slice of lemon.

Yolanda couldn't believe Andre remembered how she liked her tea. She didn't think he was listening when they talked about everything and anything under the sun during their time together. But, that was only one thing and Andre was still an unforgivable liar as far as she was concerned.

"Yolanda, I know you probably really hate me, as you have said numerous times today. And, from your perception of things, I can see why. But, you have to believe me when I say I really care about you." Andre sat down in the Queen Anne chair across from Yolanda. He wanted to hold her so bad that his heart ached, but he wouldn't dare go near her now. He didn't know what the next round would bring and he couldn't risk unleashing the beast.

"I know that things started wonderfully and ended terribly, but if you will let me explain, I will tell you everything." Andre looked over at Yolanda, waiting to hear her response and noticed that she was asleep. All of the fighting must have worn her out. Andre smiled, readjusted her blanket, and kissed her forehead. He decided to prepare a late lunch while Yolanda was sleeping. He made a killer Cobb salad with homemade blue cheese dressing and some raspberry iced tea to wash it all down.

Andre tapped Yolanda lightly on the shoulder to wake her. He chuckled silently as Yolanda awoke, looking around, trying to figure out where she was.

"Oh my God. What time is it? Timothy is going to kill me. I have got to get out of here."

"Yolanda calm down. It is only two o'clock. I've made lunch for us, so let's eat and then I can say everything that I have wanted to say." Andre gestured toward the kitchen and asked Yolanda to follow him.

"I can't stay. I have a husband at home. This relationship that we have developed is wrong, Andre. I have committed adultery, and it is something that I will have to live with the rest of my life. So, I am going, and you will never have to see me again." Yolanda walked toward the door and Andre jumped in front of her, blocking her path.

"Yolanda, I can't let you leave until you hear what I have to say." Andre held her hand firmly and led her to the couch. "I don't mean to be so frank with you, but you will listen to what I have to say before you leave today. After I have said everything, you can process the information how you want to, but I have to get this off my chest. Now, we can talk while we eat lunch. You know where everything is, so you can go freshen up in my bathroom."

Yolanda walked into the bathroom and was immediately flooded with memories. The wonderful flashback created a warm body and weak knees. So much so that she had to grip the edge of the sink to gather her composure and balance. She hurriedly washed her hands and left the bathroom, not even bothering to look at the huge Jacuzzi where the romance was conceived.

Lunch was quiet. Andre wondered what Yolanda would think of him after he told her all about his past. Yolanda was thinking of a way to tell Andre she would never see him again, no matter how bad things were at home.

After Andre refilled Yolanda's tea, he sat down and began to tell her all about his childhood. Yolanda sat with her mouth open as Andre recounted his childhood.

"My grandmother ran a liquor house. My mother was a madam. My dad left when I was young, running in and out of our lives, getting his hustle on. I ran the streets and joined a petty gang as a teen, longing for a sense of belonging. In my early twenties I started working as a bartender in a popular strip club in Atlanta, called Jewelz. One of my street buddies hooked me up with the job after getting hired as a bouncer. I worked a couple of years, and that's where I met Vicki.

We kicked it for a year before I found out that Vicki was sleeping with my first cousins, R.J. and Lamar. I began to drink heavily and needed extra money, so I began working as a stripper at another underground club. I was high on powder, and had a nice buzz the whole time, so I was never nervous or modest. I always scanned the audience looking for the lady who would spend the most money, and I usually picked the right one, and whatever she needed after the show, as long as the money was tight, she got. The money started flowing in; I stopped the drugs and drinking, and started stashing my money away. I eventually had so many ladies, I had to create a waiting list. In time, I couldn't keep up with the demand physically, if you know what I mean, so I had to stop the extra-curricular activities. So, I purchased the club. I know you are wondering how I had enough money to by a club, but this was an elite underground club. Only the crème de la crème were allowed. The club opened at midnight, and the women came in and thought nothing of dropping a few thousand for a lap dance, so you know an overnighter was mad money. Anyway, after a while, the whole lifestyle got old. I still felt something was missing in my life. I sold the business, packed up, and left the ATL. I enrolled in college, got a degree in Tele-Communications, and here I am. I know it is crazy, but it's true.

Vicki has continually harassed me, asking for forgiveness, wanting to start over. She tracks me down wherever I go. That is why she moved to South Carolina. She found out I was here through a friend, so she moved here. She searched every church, club, and gym in South Carolina until she found me.

And she probably managed to sleep with every man she has met along the way. But, she never gave up on trying to reconcile our relationship. You know Vicki is a beautiful woman with a nice figure, and she uses that to get who and what she wants. She has called, come by and continuously harassed me since then. I don't want her and never will. I will not keep moving and changing my number to get away from her; a con artist can find out the President's personal phone number if they needed it, and that's what Vicki is. But, I know what I want, and that is you Yolanda. And now, Vicki pops up again, out of nowhere, ruining my life, once again."

Yolanda had so many emotions running through her that she sat silently, wondering if Andre could possibly be telling the truth. His life story was like a work of fiction, something you would see in the movies. How could she have been attracted to a stripper? How could she not have known? Oh my God, how many women has he slept with?

"Yolanda I know that you are wondering about my status. I have been tested twice yearly for every disease possible, and I am negative. I would never risk anyone's life now that I know how precious it is. I find it hard to tell people about my past because they can't get past it. They still see me as Andre the stripper, instead of Andre the man who met Jesus. And church folk are the worst. I can't tell you how many churches have basically condemned me because I thought I could confide in the Pastors and get counseling. The men wanted me out of the church, because they thought I wanted their women, while the women wanted me to stay and be their boy toy.

This fool is crazy. How could I have gotten mixed up with him? Yolanda's thought were running wild.

"So, I was in a constant dilemma, trying to find a church where I could really get counseling. That's when I found the Redeemed Outreach Center, a place for people like me, outcasts that the mainstream churches don't want to take the time to deal with. So, I am learning about life with Jesus, one step at a time. I am not perfect in any way, but I am striving for perfection. I want to settle down and have kids, be a family man, committed to one woman."

Andre continued to talk, pouring out his heart to Yolanda, telling her all about his past and present. He did not want to withhold any information from her that could be used against him any more. She would know every detail as far back as he could remember. He would let nothing else come in to try to destroy the relationship they were building.

Yolanda listened intently as Andre doled out his life history to her, saddened that she would have to tell him that she would not be seeing him again. She knew that she would be reconciled to Timothy no matter what it took. Timothy was her husband and she could not keep using Andre to run away from her problems. Yolanda felt as if she was becoming a different woman from the passive person she once was. Everything that she had been through had empowered her to become stronger, and not let everyone run over her anymore. The kicker would be getting Timothy to see the change. She decided right then and there, that Timothy would not beat her anymore. They would have a marriage like it used to be, and even though he said she was second fiddle right now, she was going to be first, no matter what it took.

"Yolanda, are you listening to me?"

"Andre, I have to go."

"What, I pour out my soul to you and that's all you have to say?"

"Andre, I am sorry about what happened to you when you were young. I am truly sorry, but I am married and I have to concentrate on rebuilding my relationship. I came to say goodbye."

Yolanda stood and started to walk toward the door. Andre stepped in front of her, grabbed her by shoulders and looked deeply into her eyes. Not a word was spoken as he tilted her head to him and kissed her softly and deeply. Yolanda's body went limp. It was futile to fight. "I will see you again Yolanda. This is not the last time. I know it may take time, but you will be mine."

Yolanda left and drove toward her office. She decided to finish up her paperwork from Amy's visit. Anything to keep her mind off Andre. Maybe she would stop by Timothy's office and see him while she was there. It is hard for her to get in without an appointment, and she was his wife. Maybe he could make time for her today. He had to. Yolanda knew that Timothy would have to totally consume her to forget about Andre. And the way their relationship had been lately, she knew that only the good Lord could change that.

Yolanda walked toward her office to freshen up, readjusting her clothing and hair, now feeling the "A" burn itself deeper into her chest. She could still feel Andre's lips on hers. She felt someone staring at her, and looked up to see Ms. Loleather Jones, the mother of the church.

"Where you goin' in such a herry, gal?"

"I am going to my office and then I am going to see my husband, Ms. Loleather. Is there something I can help you with?"

"How you gon' hep me, when you can't even hep yosef'? I told Reverend Timothy not to marry you, 'cause you won't nothin' but trouble, but he won't listen' to me." Yolanda knew that Ms. Loleather didn't like her, but she had never come out and said so. What had transpired that made her go off like that? Yolanda knew that old people could see, and Yolanda wondered if the scarlet letter she was brandishing was shining like a neon light to Ms. Loleather.

"Ms. Loleather, what are you talking about?"

"You know what I'm talkin' 'bout. I'm talkin' 'bout that beby in yo' tummy, that's what I'm talkin' 'bout! You ain't tole nobody nuthin', so it must not be Rev's! But, don't werry, it's our secret." Yolanda stumbled at the news, knowing that old women were never wrong about pregnancy, but she couldn't let her alarm show. Oh God, what am I going to do? Yolanda could feel Ms. Loleather's squinty eyes staring right through her. Her copper toned leathery skin and wiry frame made her look just like a copperhead snake. And the long ponytail she wore braided down her back was almost as long as she was tall, which was probably about four and a half feet. Yolanda could feel the venom on her lips, waiting to spit on her like a cobra, striking out.

"Ms. Loleather, if I am pregnant, number one, I didn't know, and number two, the baby is definitely Timothy's. So you have a good day and I will keep what you said in mind. If my body

PAMELA D. RICE

changes and tells me that I have conceived a child, you will be the first to know."

Yolanda walked away, feeling Ms. Loleather's eyes continuing to sear right through her. Yolanda knew she was looking at her hips to see if they have spread, but she wouldn't dare look back. She held her head up high and marched toward her office, willing herself not to turn and look back. Now she knew how Lot's wife felt when they left Sodom and Gomorrah … just one last look. It would be fateful, just as it was with Lot's wife, so she kept walking until she walked into her office. As soon as she entered, she stumbled to the couch, fell onto it, and caught her breath. Her heart was beating so fast that she could hear the reverberations in her head. How could I be pregnant? Yolanda realized that she really hadn't thought about her period being late since there was so much drama going on in her life. She grabbed her purse and found the migraine medicine bottle and opened it. She shook out a couple of the pills and went to her mini-fridge to get bottled water. She popped the pills in her mouth and took a chug of water.

Yolanda spit the pills out quickly, choking and spewing water and saliva all over her chartreuse silk blouse. If she was pregnant, she did know that pregnant women shouldn't take aspirin products. Waves of nausea overtook her as she thought about what Ms. Loleather said, and she tried to suppress the urge to vomit. No longer able to hold the tide rhythmically building inside her, Yolanda grabbed the nearest trashcan and let it roll out. She was glad that Mary was gone, because she would have told Timothy, and she didn't need him asking her a million questions. Yolanda entered the bathroom and wet a towel for her face. She cleaned herself up, brushed her teeth, and used mouthwash to remove the awful taste in her mouth. Yolanda rewet the towel and placed it on the back of her neck, and relished in its coolness. Yolanda walked back out into her office and saw the door closing out of the corner of her eyes. She knew that it was nosy Ms. Loleather. Yolanda could not believe that she had followed her and tried to spy on her. She didn't care; she just wanted to lie down. Yolanda locked her door, plopped down on her couch, put her legs up for a minute, and gathered her composure. Yolanda decided to just wait to see Timothy later. After the bombshell Ms. Loleather dropped, she didn't think she could face Timothy just yet.

CHAPTER 14

Yolanda greeted Timothy with a kiss as he entered the kitchen. Even though she didn't love him deep down, she had to try to salvage her marriage. That would be the Godly thing to do.

"Yolanda, what's wrong with you? Why are you acting so fresh?" "Can't a woman be happy to see her husband?" Yolanda placed her arms around Timothy's neck and tried to kiss him on the cheek. Timothy removed her arms from around his neck and headed to the stove.

"What's for dinner, I'm hungry."

"We are having grilled chicken from Ruby Tuesday's and I placed them in the warmer, so wash up and we'll be ready." Yolanda reached into the cabinet to get glasses for the tea she had prepared earlier. Suddenly, she felt the wave of nausea show its ugly head once again. It had to be in her head. She was never nauseous until Ms. Loleather said she was pregnant.

"Why is it so hard to get a home cooked meal around here?" Even though Yolanda could tell that Timothy was agitated, she could not go back on the promise she made to empower herself. She had to find a way to keep him calm. "Timothy..." Just then another wave tossed itself in the sea of acid in her stomach, and churned her insides. Yolanda grabbed the countertop, put her head down and held on for the ride.

"What's wrong with you? I know you aren't trying to catch an attitude with me, or are you calling yourself tuning me out?" Yolanda used her hands to find her way to the kitchen table, daring her body to spill any of its contents in front of Timothy, which would spark a barrage of insults over how she tried to ruin his appetite.

"Don't try to act like you sick, because that won't work, either!"

"Timothy, I am fine, I think it's just been a long day and I overexerted myself in this heat. Maybe I will go lie down and then I will eat later. But, you can eat now. I know that you are hungry." Yolanda turned to go upstairs, but Timothy grabbed her arm.

"Yolanda, maybe you didn't hear me. I said I need a home-cooked meal. I am not eating this slop that's filled with who knows what!" Timothy grabbed his plate from the warmer and dumped it in the trashcan.

"Now, you cook me some real food. I want some lasagna tonight."

"Timothy, what has happened to you?" Yolanda let the tears flow freely as she began to wring her hands.

"You never used to treat me this way. Now, I can't do anything to please you. You have told me I was second in your life, and you have resorted to physically assaulting me! Being a Psychologist, I can tell that your behavior is rooted in something that has you unsettled. There has been a major change in your life and you feel that someone has to be your whipping post...." Yolanda didn't even see the fist coming and it lands squarely against her jaw. Intense pain shot through her, and the lights went dim.

Yolanda awoke the next morning in bed with her black baby doll top lingerie and no bottoms. Her head hurt and her bladder felt like it was about to overflow. She sat on the edge of the bed and the lightning bolt of pain hits her exactly where Timothy had hit her the night before. Yolanda made her way to the bathroom to let the floodwaters pass. As she wiped herself, she wiped away a part of Timothy also. He had taken advantage of her once again.

When Timothy left, Yolanda took a long hot shower. She slowly washed her body and washed away any signs of him. After she showered, Yolanda rubbed her body down with Shea butter and put on her robe. She called Mary, and asked her to reschedule her appointments for the day due to illness. After assuring Mary that she was fine, that it was probably just a virus, Yolanda hung up the phone and went downstairs to make some tea.

As Yolanda sipped her tea, she planned her day. She would stop by Timothy's office and ask him for a divorce. Then she would go to Walgreen's in Greenville and buy a pregnancy test. She couldn't risk anyone from church seeing her, even though they had a few parishioners make the drive to Sparkle City from Greenville. If she was pregnant, she didn't know who the father was, and she couldn't risk Timothy finding out until she was sure.

Yolanda walked down the corridor to Timothy's office, wiping her sweaty palms on the hands of her skirt. She was wearing a traditional A-line black skirt, with a white button-down blouse and peep-toe pumps. Her hair was pulled neatly back into a bun, very business-like, and she knew the business she needed to handle. I am empowered! I am the head and not the tail! I can do all things through Christ, which strengthens me…Yolanda felt odd quoting scripture to God about the husband she wanted to divorce; the same husband to which she promised "till death do us part". Even though she felt that God thought she was wishy-washy, she knew that He did not want her to stay in a relationship where she was being physically abused. And, she couldn't go to counseling with her pastor, because she was married to him. Forget telling anyone else, it would be on the front of the Herald Journal and News Channel Seven. Yolanda took a deep breath, repeated her mantra, and knocked three times. She still couldn't believe she had to knock on her own husband's door.

"Yolanda, what brings you here?" Timothy stepped back to let Yolanda come inside.

"Timothy, why are you sweating? Are you feeling alright?" Yolanda was concerned looking at Timothy. He was wild eyed, and appeared to be nervous. "Is everything alright?" Yolanda noticed the hold light flashing on Timothy's phone and asked who was on the other line. Timothy picked up the phone and told the person on the line that he would return their call later. Obviously agitated, Timothy yelled in the phone that he knew hat his responsibilities were. He slammed the phone down and looked at Yolanda.

"I said what are you doing here?"

"Timothy, who was that on the phone?" What is going on, what I have to say can wait."

"Oh, I forgot, Mrs. Psychologist, you can solve everyone's problems. You know everything." Yolanda coiled at the insults being hurled at her. The hurt that Timothy spit felt like cinder blocks tumbling down on her.

"Why do you hate me so much now, Timothy? I have done nothing but love and support you all of our life together, and you treat me like dirt. Why?"

"You make me sick because you think you know everything. You have an answer for all of life's mysteries." Yolanda stood looking at Timothy, filled with pure hatred.

"I am so tired of trying to teach you to be submissive. I have wasted too much energy on you. Your inheritance is the only reason I haven't dumped you. It has helped me build this wonderful church." Timothy wiped his brow.

"There is certainly nothing else that you can offer me that's good, especially in the bedroom. You have no passion. I just sleep with you to relieve the stress of everyday life. Maybe you should see a shrink and find where it's is hidden. Maybe they can dig it out of you and help you find it." Yolanda looked Timothy directly in the eye, wondering how he could belittle her womanhood when he had just raped her again last night.

"You don't have to worry about even looking at me anymore Timothy. I want a divorce." Yolanda spoke softly, and her voice was as weak as a kitten's meow.

"What did you say?" Yolanda held onto the back of the burgundy wing chair to steady her now wobbly legs. I am empowered…. "Timothy if you don't love me, and you hate

106

me…then there is no need to pretend anymore. I'm glad you were honest about your feelings, even though you have wounded me to the core. We are both adults, so we can communicate like adults. I will have my lawyer draw up the paperwork for the divorce so that you won't have to tolerate me anymore." The rage in Timothy's eyes seemed to hold Yolanda in a trance. She knew that she should move and take cover, but she was frozen like a deer in headlights.

"Do you think that I will ever divorce you? I will lose everything that I have worked so hard to build. This church is my life, and I am not going to lose it over a pathetic woman like you. If you ever try to leave me, I will kill you- that is a promise." Timothy lunged at Yolanda and she screamed and grabbed the door to run away. Just as she opened the door, Deacon Elton Johnson was running toward the door.

"Is everything alright in here? I heard yellin' and I came runnin'."

"Everything is fine, Deacon Johnson, Pastor Clarke was just going over his sermon for Sunday. He just got excited about the word he had." Yolanda didn't know or care if the deacon believed her or not, she was just glad that he saved her from the stomp she was about to get.

"I'll see you later honey." Yolanda mustered a fake smile and waved the pageant wave to Timothy. She closed the door to the office, exhaling as she used the door to brace herself. She could hear Deacon Johnson hitting Timothy with a barrage of questions, and knew that Timothy the mole would dig his way out of the hole.

Walgreen's wasn't crowded and Yolanda was glad. She hurriedly purchased the pregnancy test and almost ran into the restroom, anxious for an answer. She followed the directions and waited, praying not to see a plus sign. She felt stupid and angry as she remembered every hurtful word Timothy said. She held her breath, crossed her fingers and prayed. She looked at her watch. Two minutes exactly, and no plus sign. Thank God. Yolanda wanted to kiss the stick, but thought about the body fluid she had just deposited on it. She laughed out loud, and took one last look for good measure, and saw a faint blue plus sign smile at her. Yolanda became woozy and held onto the walls of the stall for support. She purchased two more pregnancy tests from "Lisa" the cashier, who was perturbed that her personal phone conversation kept getting interrupted. Yolanda could no longer deny the truth. She was pregnant.

Yolanda dialed four-one-one to get the number to her gynecologist so that she could schedule an appointment. She made sure that any changes to her appointment would be relayed by cell phone only. No calls were to come to her home. Thank God for the new HIPPA laws, which protected patients' privacy. Her appointment was in two weeks, and she couldn't wait to update her form. Yolanda called the church and asked to speak with Timothy. She had to make sure that he was still there before she went into the house, since he was so angry with her earlier.

"What do you want Yolanda? I am not going to get my sermon written if you keep bugging me."

"I just called to see what you wanted for dinner, that's all. Don't worry, I will be creative and make something special. Bye."

Yolanda arrived home, and checked the mailbox, which was crammed full, door partially opened. She and Timothy always forgot the mail. Yolanda started to separate the mail as she walked to Timothy's office to place his mail on his desk. As she hurried through the stack, something caught her eye. It was an envelope addressed to Timothy from Piedmont Urology. Yolanda had never opened Timothy's mail, (he had forbidden her), but her curiosity was piqued. She opened the letter and almost fainted when she read the contents.

Dear Mr. Timothy Clarke,
Our office has made repeated attempts to contact you… six month follow-up for your vasectomy… Please be advised…

Yolanda stared at the letter in disbelief, reading it again and again. She placed the rest of the mail on his desk, and plopped down in his chair, laughing out loud, knowing that someone would hop out and tell her she's on television or something. After she could laugh no longer, Yolanda broke down crying, wondering how she had put up with Timothy for ten years. She thought about how he said she couldn't have kids because she wasn't submissive, or because her nipples were inverted, along with a million other reasons. All the insults and jabs she'd endured from Timothy, too afraid to tell someone, too afraid to leave. Well now was payback time. The old saying about a woman scorned was true. Yolanda was about to send Timothy on a slow train to Hell.

CHAPTER 15

Time seemed to stand still and Yolanda was unsuccessfully trying to get back into the swing of things at work. She was terribly depressed and felt like she only had two things to live for. Her unborn child and getting back at Timothy. She had transferred all of her patients to another doctor. She was cleaning out her office and transferring files electronically, which would take her several more weeks to complete.

Yolanda thought about her baby and wondered what kind of nursery pattern she would choose. She had looked online at several different styles, but could not make a decision. She also had been out with a Realtor several times, trying to find a small home for her and her unborn child. Yolanda had no desire to try to patch things up with Timothy. What he did to her was worse than anything she could ever have imagined, and she would never forgive him for it. She made sure she walked on eggshells around him at home all the time, trying her best not to get in his way. She did not want to risk him harming her child in any way.

Yolanda knew that she needed to tell Andre that he was the father of her child. She still had feelings for him, as strange as it was, but the timing had never felt right. She would have to tell him soon, though, he deserved to know.

Yolanda sat in the beauty shop, listening to all the gossip, trying do decide how she wanted her hair styled. She decided on a sexy upsweep, with a few wispy bangs. The sweltering summer heat ravaged everyone's hair. Summer in South Carolina was no joke; it was comparable to the fiery furnace. Yolanda snickered to herself as she listened to her hairdresser Arlene talk about Deacon Ponds and his wife's marital problems. They attended the Missionary COGIC down the street. Arlene stopped wrapping her hair, to tell the story with her hands. "Deacon Ponds was having an affair, and his wife found out about it. So, she put Nair hair remover in his shampoo, and you know what happened. He went to the barbershop, fussing at the barbers, looking like a mangy puppy when his hair started falling out in patches." The beauty shop erupted in laughter and Arlene shushed everyone so that she could finish the story. "That's not all; she also purchased some itching powder online, and sprinkled it in all his underwear. Ya'll know that man was walking around scratching himself, and looking crazy." Everyone in the shop was laughed out loud, including Yolanda. She made mental notes of items she needed to purchase.

Yolanda was starving by the time she left Arlene's and she headed straight to McDonalds. A plain cheeseburger, small fry, and ice water would hold her until she could get dinner cooked. She cooked dinner every night for Timothy now, not wanting to feel his wrath.

After eating her snack, Yolanda headed to the Fresh Market to get some salmon steaks, fresh pasta, and broccoli. She tried to limit her fish to twice weekly after reading all of the stories and pregnant mothers and mercury ingestion. Her phone rang and it was Andre. She didn't answer, but listened to the voice mail. "Hey Yolanda, I just wanted to check in to see how you were doing. Call me when you get this message." Andre had left her many messages, but she could never call him back. Her nerves were too raw and her wounds too fresh. Besides, she had to put all of her energy into getting back at Timothy.

Yolanda arrived at her house and kicked her shoes off. She stalled at her prayer closet. She needed to go in and seek the Lord, but didn't want Him telling her she was headed down the wrong path with her plans for revenge. Maybe tomorrow...

Dinner was complete and the table was set when Timothy arrived home. "Yolanda, I am glad that you are finally starting to see things my way, and that you have finally learned what submission really means." Yolanda flinched inside as she smiled at Timothy, when she really wanted to gouge his eyes out instead. Everything in due time.

Another day at work and Yolanda was still transferring her files and cleaning out her office. The process would have gone faster if she could have concentrated, and stopped thinking about Timothy. She started to worry, knowing her revenge on him was clouding her every waking moment. But, she couldn't help it; he had to hurt as much as she was.

Yolanda called Amy and checked in on her. It had been a couple of weeks since she had spoken with her.

"Hi, how are things going with your new counselor?"
"They are alright, but no one can ever replace you. You know that."

"Thanks Amy, I appreciate that, but, I need to clear some things up in my own life before I am able to help someone else."

"Mrs. Yolanda, you know if you need to talk to someone, you can trust me."

"I know Amy, but there are some things that you can only tell Jesus. Hey, how about we go and grab a bite to eat?"

"I'm sorry Mrs. Yolanda, J.R. and I are going to Pizza Inn for buffet. But, you can join us."

"No thanks Amy, a third wheel still can't balance a car. You guys have fun." Yolanda sat at her desk, feeling lonely. She realized that she had no friends. Her relationship with her parents had been strained for years because of her marriage to Timothy. Vicki only pretended to be her friend to get her claws into Timothy. Andre came in and destroyed her life, and even he knew Timothy. Everything led back to Timothy. He was the root of all her problems. Yolanda realized how much she hated him. She broke down crying, and decided to call it a day. Her emotions were out of whack because of the pregnancy. She was reading a book that documented each stage of pregnancy, and was amazed at how closely the book mirrored her own.

Yolanda arrived home and headed straight to her closet to change clothes. Even though she knew she should step in and say a quick prayer, there was no time. She had to get the Nair into Timothy's shampoo bottle before he arrived home. She made sure she purchased the new "no scent" brand. After maneuvering the bottles, Yolanda finally transferred the contents. She wiped the shampoo bottle clean and smiled, proud of herself. She went back to her closet and reached onto the top shelf, still not praying while there, and removed the itching powder. She scooped up every pair of Timothy's underwear and spread them on the deck. One by one, she gave each one a dusting and shook the excess out.   She was so glad that her back yard was lined with trees that acted as a privacy fence. She wouldn't want anyone to see her. Yolanda refolded the underwear and placed it back into the drawers. The mask, gloves and long sleeves she wore protected her, and after she finished, she bagged them up and disposed of them.

It was Sunday morning, and Yolanda scrambled to find something to wear to church. She selected a sage green suit from her closet. She hadn't worn it in a while and always received compliments on how well the color matched her skin tone. She was so glad that Timothy had already left; it gave her time to get dressed in peace. Yolanda started toward the closet to retrieve the matching hat. She knew that she should go in and pray, but wouldn't, even though conviction was on her to do so. Timothy had to get his just reward. He deserved everything he was going to get, and then some.

The choir was entering the sanctuary as Yolanda arrived. She was so glad that Timothy was still in his office. He hated when she came in so close to service starting. After the last TKO, she was not trying to get in his way. Yolanda seated herself and wrote out a check for her tithes and offering. She may have been an adulteress, a plotter of evil towards Timothy, but she was not going to have another curse over her life by withholding money from God. That was serious business. Yolanda felt someone staring at her and looked over her shoulder. "Oh, hi Vicki. How are you today?" Vicki didn't say a word. She just looked at Yolanda like she was crazy. Yolanda smiled inside and turned around, almost swearing she saw Vicki tremble. I am empowered, she thought to herself. Yolanda knew that she had won the battle and wouldn't have to worry about Vicki saying to Timothy about Andre. She refused to be a victim of circumstance anymore. Vicki passed her a note.

Don't blame Dre. He didn't know I was coming. He cool. He care for you.

Yolanda stared at the note, then crumpled it and put it in her purse. How can she be a secretary with writing skills like this? Yolanda dismissed her own stupidity, knowing that it wasn't Vicki's writing skills that landed her the job. She would have to remember to get rid of the note before going home.

The choir was exuberant, and Yolanda stood up and joined in singing with them, waving her hands in the air and singing. "This is the day, that the Lord has made, I will rejoice..." Everyone repeated the leader and the whole church was rocking. People were in the aisles greeting one another, and having a good time. Timothy came out and looked over the congregation. Normally, he would have used the opportunity to rev up the congregation more, but he looked uncomfortable. He sat down and Yolanda noticed him squirming in the chair. As he walked to the podium, Yolanda noticed that his hands brush the front of his robe. He stepped to the podium and motioned for William, the Assistant Pastor, to come up. He whispered in his ear and Pastor William took over the services as Timothy left the pulpit. Yolanda immediately walked out and met Timothy as he walked toward his office. "Is everything alright, Timothy?" Yolanda put her hand on his arm, feigning concern. They walked into his office and closed the door. Timothy spoke softly.

"Have you switched to a different detergent or something? The last few days, my privates have been itching terribly." He yanked off the robe and scratched himself violently.

"No, I haven't, but if I had, don't you think it would be more than your privates bothering you?" Yolanda gave him a serious "what have you been doing look", and Timothy turned away. Immediately he thought about Vicki. He knew that he might run into trouble messing with her, especially without condoms.

"Drive me home, we'll come back and get your car. I don't want the congregation to know what's wrong. I will tell them I have a virus or something."

Yolanda tried not to fall out laughing as she drove Timothy home. She bet he had no skin left on his privates, as much as he'd scratched.

When they arrived home, Timothy jumped into the shower, and welcomed the relief of the cool water. While he was in the shower, Yolanda carefully removed his underwear from his drawer and threw them in a trash bag, along with Vicki's ripped up note. She wiped his drawer down with Clorox wipes and allowed it to air dry. When Timothy got out of the shower, he didn't say a word. He put on his robe, and nothing else. "I am going to the mall, to buy some underwear for you. Also, I will schedule a doctor's appointment for you tomorrow." Timothy looked away, still not saying anything. Yolanda walked out with the trash bag, dumped it in the bin and headed to her car. Yolanda laughed out loud, and realized that guilt could make you believe anything.

A couple of weeks go by and Yolanda wondered if Timothy's hair was coming out yet. She tried to sneak a peek as he walked by, not wanting to draw his attention. She thought she could see small thinning patches, but it was probably only her high hopes. She was still cooking every day, the content wife, waiting for her chance to pounce.

CHAPTER 16

Yolanda walked into the doctor's office and hoped she wouldn't have to wait long. She told Timothy that she was going for her yearly physical and then to visit her parents. The alibi would provide her ample time if she needed it.

She was soon called to the lab. The small lancet the lab technician used left her fingertip sore, and she figured she must have more nerve endings than most people. After getting her vitals, labs and weight, Yolanda was escorted into an exam room where she waited. Today she would be having an ultrasound, and she was nervous, but excited. The ultrasound technician came into the room and prepared Yolanda for the ultrasound.

"Hi, I'm Deanna, and I will be taking care of you today." Deanna explained everything she was going to do before starting the procedure. The warm liquid felt good on her belly. Deanna rubbed the probe over her belly searching for the baby. She pointed out a tiny bean shape.

"This is the baby, and it has a strong heartbeat." Yolanda looked at the screen, unable to believe that a baby was actually growing inside her. She was feeling a range of emotions; happy and sad at the same time. Happy because she finally would be a mother, something that she had longed for. Sad, because she had no one to share her moment with. She knew that she would have to tell Andre before the day was over. He deserved to know that he was going to be a father.

After her visit, Yolanda called Andre. He picked up immediately.

"Hi, I've been waiting for you to call. I didn't want to give up on you. I have spent weeks trying to forget about you, but I can't. I wonder if you are thinking about me. I am not obsessed, I know that we will be together, but I just don't know how it will work…"

"Andre." Yolanda hated to interrupt, but she had to talk before she lost her nerve.

"I need to talk to you. Can I come over?"

"Sure, I'll make lunch"

"No, I'm in the mood for Thai, and I have already ordered it. Is that okay with you?"

"Yes, that sounds great."

"See ya soon."

When Yolanda arrived, the garage door was already up and Yolanda pulled in. Andre was at her door smiling before she could even get out. Yolanda hated that smile. It still captivated her.

"Wow, you look great!" Andre grabbed her and hugged her, resting his head on her shoulder. Yolanda nudged him lightly.

"We better eat before the food gets cold." She headed into the kitchen. Andre asked her a million questions as they chowed down on basil fried rice, steamed dumplings, and pad Thai. Yolanda tried to keep the answers short and sweet, so that she could give him the news before she lost her nerve. He also showed her his "papers" proving that he was still disease free.

"Andre, I can't stay long, I have got to get back to the office. There is something that I need to tell you. Can we go sit on the couch?" Yolanda sat down and started wringing her hands together, nervous at the thought of telling Andre about the pregnancy.

"You remember when we made love?"

"How could I forget? That was one of the most special moments of my life. I had been celibate for years, vowing not to sleep with another woman until I found "the one." Of course I remember; it's all I think about."

"Remember when the condom broke and we didn't realize it until it was too late?" Yolanda reached into her purse and handed Andre the picture of the ultrasound.

"What is this?" Andre stared at the glob of something on the paper.

"It's a baby…" Andre's eyes widened in disbelief.

"A baby?" Yolanda watched as an array of emotions played over Andre's face. Finally, a face of confusion settled there. "Yolanda, I would love nothing more than to be the father of your child. But, how can you be sure it's mine? After all, you are married." Yolanda stirred in her seat, wondering how she would tell Andre that her husband had a vasectomy without her knowledge.

"Timothy is unable to have children." Yolanda could not bear to tell him the whole truth. How sorry would that make her look?

"You mean this really is my child?" Andre stared at the picture for what seemed an eternity. Andre put the picture on the table and leaned over and pulled Yolanda towards him. He held her like she was a fragile egg and caressed her hair and face. He kissed her tenderly on the lips. Yolanda knew that she should pull back; her mind was telling her to. The Holy Spirit that she had been ignoring was beckoning her strongly to get up and leave. But, her body welcomed Andre's kisses; his hands that caressed her shoulders and made her spine tingle. Her mind knew that she should not give in, but her body begged to differ. Yolanda closed her eyes and relaxed, and received the tender loving care that Andre gave. All of her problems and concerns flew out the window momentarily as she and Andre became one.

"You know that we need to get married right? Andre wrapped a strand of Yolanda's hair around his finger, loving the texture.

"You know that I'm already married right?

"You can get a divorce, right?"

"Andre, it's not that simple. We both know that we still have a long way to go in getting to know each other. You know that I am an abused wife. I know that you are a former stripper and strip club owner. We both know that we have unbelievable chemistry together, and that's about it. I will not jump into another marriage, even if the lovin' is better than anything I could ever imagine."

"Well, I know that I do not want to spend another moment alone. I know that I want to take care of you and my child. I know that I want to spend the rest of my life with you, and that's all I need to know. I am not going to let you go back to that house and risk Timothy hurting you or my child!" Yolanda noticed Andre's anger-edged voice rising.

"Andre, you know that I have to go home. Nobody knows that I am pregnant except my gynecologist and you. And some old lady at church..." Yolanda told Andre all about Ms. Loleather.

"Anyway, I have to go home. What would it look like if word was on the street that a pastor's wife was pregnant by and ex-stripper?"

"Why do I have to continue to be an ex-stripper? That was a long time ago. I have changed, so why do you keep bringing up the past? Don't tell me you're really like all the rest of the church folk. You don't bring up your past, but you love to remind everyone else about who they were, and what they did."

"Andre, calm down. I'm sorry if I offended you, that was not my intention. I know that you are a changed person. If you were not, I would not be here. I never would have imagined that you were ever a stripper. I was just saying..."

"Well, just say a pastor's wife is pregnant by another fellow Christian. That sounds so much better than ex-stripper."

"Well, you know that if the story ever comes out, we'll both be classified as heathens. Everyone will ask, "How can two Christians fall? How can two people who know right from wrong make such a tragic mistake?"

"I don't know, Yolanda. But, I do know this. I am going to be the best father in the whole world to my child. I didn't have the best childhood, so I will give my life to make it better for my child." Yolanda didn't say another word; she just remained quiet, deep in thought.

CHAPTER 17

Yolanda called Timothy as soon as she left Andre's home. "What do you want Yolanda? I am in a meeting."

"I just called to see if you would be home for dinner."

"No. I will be home after tonight's services." Yolanda was glad. It was four o'clock, and that would give her time to put some chicken, rice and veggies in the crock pot. If she cooked it on high, it would be ready by the time they returned home. Yolanda was exhausted from the day's extracurricular activities, but knew that missing the midweek service was not an option. She hurried home, showered and dressed, threw dinner on, and left. As soon as she was seated, Ms. Loleather began to pray. *God, if I knew she was going to teach.....*

"Today's lesson will be comin' from second Samuel the eleventh chapter. We gone be talkin' about David and Bathsheba, and the consequences they faced for their adulterous relationship. I know this is not what you all studied and prepared for, but I feel the Lord leading me in this direction. Amen?"

"Mother you go wit' the Lord."

"Preach Mama!"

Yolanda looked at Ms. Loleather and felt squinty eyes that threatened to cut her to shreds staring at her. They played a game of stare down, until Yolanda looked down. Ms. Loleather laughed and said something about the devil trying to disrupt the services. I am empowered through Christ Jesus who strengthens me...

Timothy came and sat down next to her so fast, it caught her off guard. She felt the muscles tense in her neck, and wondered if he could tell she had been intimate with Andre earlier.

"Now er 'body always wants to blame David for what he did. But, that woman Bathsheba knew what she wuz doin' when she was out there on that roof wit' no clothes on in plain day. She wuz tryin' to entice him, cuz' her own husband wuz away workin', fightin' in a war. She probly felt like he won't payin' her 'nuf 'tention, cuz he was tryin' to do what he wuz called to do. That's how some of these church wives is. They husbands be tryin' to do church work, and they wives is never satisfied. Dese mens be workin' hard for the Lawd, and dese womens just be complainin'. They have the best mens in the world, but they jest can't be satisfied. Bathsheba got satisfied, and ended up pregnant, and ya'll folks know what I mean by satisfied. But, you know what happened to Bathsheba for carryin' another man's child? The beby died."

Yolanda felt as if the air around her was trying to squeeze the life out of her, and struggled to catch her breath. I am empowered... Yolanda cleared her throat and spoke.

"Ms. Loleather, even though their baby died, they stayed together because they obviously loved one another. And even though both of them sinned, God forgave them and blessed them with another child named Solomon and the Lord loved him. As for David, God went on to say that he was a man after his own heart, so when the head got right, everyone else fell in line. Out of the ashes of their sin, God brought forth the greatest sin bearer of all times, who was Jesus Christ. So, even though their adulterous relationship, which was a small seed, brought forth a harvest of great consequences- lies, betrayal, and death; God still forgave them and blessed them with eternal life."

Everyone was looking at Yolanda, totally stunned by her outburst. They knew that she never talked in any of the services, and hearing her make a comment about anything was unheard of.

Ms. Loleather stared at Yolanda and laughed a deep belly laugh, but Yolanda would not look down. Yolanda felt that she no longer had to take the abuse that she dished out to her every week. Yolanda understood the principle behind respecting elders, but this had gone far enough. She figured that Ms. Loleather had forgotten about her days as abortionist. She used to charge young mothers twenty dollars back in the day to perform crude abortions on them, so they would not have to walk around in shame. Yolanda would have never known about it if one of the members hadn't come to her for counseling.

Moneree Martin had come to her because she could not come to terms with the abortion that she'd had over forty-five years ago, when she was a senior in high school. She found out that she was pregnant after the year-end school dance, and she wanted to go to college. Her boyfriend at the time, Wilbur, was working at a local mill, and scraped up enough money for her to have the procedure. Moneree told Yolanda that it was hard for her to forgive herself for having an abortion, and she still felt uneasy about seeing Ms. Loleather every week, wondering if she would tell someone about her past. Yolanda assured Moneree that Ms. Loleather would not tell anyone, because she would have to bring her own skeletons out of the closet.

Yolanda had hoped and prayed that Ms. Loleather had learned not to judge others, but it was obvious that she hadn't. Yolanda could not believe that Ms. Loleather was trying to call her out in front of everyone, like she had never sinned in her life. Yolanda stared back at her, not even blinking, daring her to say another word, because if she had, Yolanda decided that she would mention that Bathsheba could have opted for an abortion. Then she would ask her if that would have been a bigger sin. She was sure the sister would get her drift then because no one liked to be exposed.

"If there be no more comments, we gone move on." Ms. Loleather started reading from the Bible in second Samuel about David.

PAMELA D. RICE

Yolanda excused herself and went to her office. She knew that Timothy would be enraged with her for leaving in the middle of the service, but she just could not take anymore. She settled in on her couch and started perusing the latest issue of a Christian magazine. Timothy barged in the door.

"What the heck is wrong with you Yolanda? Have you lost your ever-lovin' mind? What's up with that little stunt you just pulled out there? Do you know how many people were looking at me when you left? You are getting' to big for your britches again, and I think you need another lesson in submission!" Timothy grabbed Yolanda harshly and pulled her towards him. His face was so close to hers that their eyelashes touched.

"This beating is going to be one that you can tell your grandchildren about. Oh, I forgot, you could not even get pregnant! You are pathetic! I am not even going to waste my energy on you." Timothy forcefully pushed Yolanda back down on the couch. A knock on the door snapped Timothy out of his rage. He opened the door, and Deacon Johnson was standing there.

"Hey, Deac, my wife isn't feeling so well. I have to come and check on my baby, you know. Honey, are you sure that you will be able to drive yourself home?" Yolanda nodded, wondering how someone could flip from evil to pleasant so quickly. Timothy retrieved a bottle of water from her fridge and handed it to her.

"Can I get you something else, sweetie?" Yolanda looked at him like he was crazy.

"I'm good, Timothy."

"Mrs. Clarke, are you sure you're okay?" Deacon Johnson stood in the door, looking a little uneasy.

"I'm fine Deacon Johnson, thanks." Yolanda sipped the water slowly, evading eye contact with him.

"I'll see you later, sweetheart." Timothy said as he shuffled out the door, pushing Deacon Johnson along with him. Yolanda sat for a few minutes more, and then decided to head home. She knew that she was safe tonight. Timothy could tell that Deacon Johnson was looking at him sideways, and he would not take the risk of even touching her. Yolanda was glad that he saw through Timothy's little charade. Yolanda whispered a little prayer.

"Thank you Lord for letting Deacon Johnson stay at church twenty-four seven." Yolanda felt funny praying to God after she just left Andre, but God knew her heart.

After arriving home, Yolanda decided to check in with her parents. "Hi, Mom. How are you and dad doing?"

"Hi Yolanda, we are great. How are you doing? Is everything alright?" Yolanda was ashamed that her parents thought that something had to be wrong for her to call. Yolanda heard her mom whisper to her father that she was on the line.

"Nothing's wrong mom. I just called to check on you two. It's been a while since I last saw you, and I don't want to wait too long to talk to you or see you both again, that's all."

"Well honey, you know that anytime you need to talk, or if you ever want to stop by, the door is always open. Do you need anything?"

Yes, I need to tell you both that you are going to be grandparents. Yolanda thought it, but couldn't manage to say it.

"No, mom, I just called to tell you guys hello and that I love you both."

"We love you too, Yolanda. Are you sure you're alright?"

"Yes, mom, I'll come see you both soon, okay? Goodnight." Yolanda hung up and tried unsuccessfully to hold in the tears. She could not even share the news with her parents. Yolanda thought about her dismal situation. She was having a baby by another man, willfully continuing to commit adultery, and avoided her prayer closet like the plague. She thought aloud.

"Does a person like me, who really knows God, have a chance? How did I arrive at this place? Can God still love me? I am tired of the abuse Lord. I just want someone to love me. Is that so bad? I know that he is cheating on me anyway." Yolanda drifted off to sleep on the couch, too exhausted to go upstairs to bed.

Timothy shook Yolanda from a wonderful dream where she was holding her beautiful baby, rocking him gently. "Go to bed." Yolanda jumped up quickly, almost running to the bedroom. If Timothy did not wake her with a punch, it was a good sign that she would escape his violence. She was grateful once again that Deacon Johnson had an opportunity to hear one of Timothy's rants.

Yolanda slept until ten in the morning. The previous day's lovemaking session with Andre had finally caught up with her. She lay in the bed, thinking about her life and her future. She wondered what her baby would look like. Would the baby love her as much as she loved it? What would Timothy do when he found out that she was pregnant?

CHAPTER 18

Yolanda arrived at her office and slumped down in her chair. She had a couple more files to transfer, and then she could concentrate on cleaning out her office. Surprisingly, Timothy hadn't said much about her quitting, and she was grateful. Of course, he had already hinted around that he expected her to serve in some other capacity in the church. Yolanda wanted so badly to tell him that she would not be around much longer, but realized that would not be a good idea.

Lunchtime arrived quickly and Yolanda headed to Atlanta Bread. It was only eleven o'clock but she was so hungry. She ordered a veggie sandwich and a small cup of chicken noodle soup. Just as she finished, her cell phone rang. "Yolanda, this is Samantha King. How are you today? I'm waiting at my office to show you a couple of houses. Did you forget about our appointment?" "Samantha, I am so sorry! I forgot all about it. I will be there in ten minutes." Yolanda hurriedly dumped her tray and headed out to meet Samantha. She was glad that her office was close by.

The first house they toured was a small, quaint house on a cul-de-sac. It was located in the historic Converse Heights neighborhood. The house had extensive crown molding that was original along with a beautiful fireplace. The two bedrooms were fairly large and the master bedroom had a half bath. Yolanda loved the heavy wood doors and glass door knobs located throughout the house. The wood floors had been refurbished and looked absolutely amazing. The kitchen was bright white, and airy, with Jenn-Air appliances. Yolanda took a peek at the back yard and loved the koi pond and garden, and fenced in yard. This could be home...

The next house was located in a newer subdivision. It was half brick, half vinyl siding and Yolanda did not even want to look at it. She thought it was ugly.

"Yolanda, these are the only two houses I have in the price range you gave me. What did you think about the home in Converse Heights?"

"I absolutely loved it and I would like to make an offer." Yolanda was sure that the buyer would accept her offer, especially with the crummy housing market.

"Well, let's just run the pre-approval to see if you are qualified. I'm glad you filled out the paperwork already. I will send it in as soon as I get back to the office."

"Thanks, Samantha. I'll be waiting to hear from you." Samantha had to convince Yolanda to fill out the paperwork for the pre-approval process. She had to promise Yolanda that she would hold on to it until she found a home that she liked. Yolanda only complied because she was a long term friend. Yolanda did not want to take a chance on Timothy finding out anything about her planned move. She had to play her cards right.

A couple of weeks passed, and Yolanda had not heard from Samantha. She decided to give her a call.

"Samantha speaking, how can I help you?"

"Samantha, this is Yolanda Clarke. I was calling to check on the status of my loan approval."

"Yes, I was just about to call you. I am sorry to say that you have been denied the loan. However, we may be able to find some houses in a lower price range that may suit you. We have some wonderful starter homes and a few patio homes that we could probably put you in."

"I don't understand. Are you sure that you ran the right numbers? My aunt left me an inheritance, and I should not have a problem qualifying for any loan."

"Yolanda, maybe you should speak with your financial advisor. He or she should be able to direct you as how to proceed. Call me if you are interested in looking at any of the other homes I mentioned. Thanks, and have a great day."

Yolanda hung up the phone. How could I not qualify? Yolanda cannot remember the last time that she had checked the balance of the savings account. Timothy always took care of the bills and the budget. The only time she saw the balance of the checking account was when she withdrew money from the ATM. There was always plenty of money in the checking account, so she assumed that the savings was alright. Surely, Timothy could not have spent her auntie's inheritance without her knowing it. He could not be that crazy. Yolanda was ashamed that she had let Timothy control her life and that she had no knowledge about her own finances. She headed straight to the bank.

"Welcome to Bank of America, how can I help you?" Yolanda tried to smile at the bubbly blonde behind the counter, but it was hard.

"Hi, I need to get a printout of all my account balances, please." Yolanda gave "bubbly" all of the necessary information and received a printout in minutes. She took it, thanked "bubbly" and left, not even glancing at the papers. She drove home, afraid to look.

Yolanda sat in the car in the garage, and finally looked at the papers. Checking balance: twelve thousand dollars. That was right. Money market balance... was okay. IRA...okay. Savings...

Yolanda stared blankly at the paper in front of her. Surely, there had to be a typo. There was a balance of only one hundred thousand dollars. How in God's name had Timothy spent all her money? Yolanda crumpled the papers and gave the steering wheel the beat down that she wished was Timothy. She screamed, cried, and yelled. She cursed Timothy with all that she had, hoping that he would drop dead. What else could he do to her? He was an abusive husband. He was having a long term affair with her former friend. He had a vasectomy without her knowledge, and now he had spent all of her money. Yolanda wanted to march right into his office and shoot him point blank in the head.

Yolanda struggled to make herself go inside the house. She wanted to light a match and burn it all down with Timothy inside, erasing any memory of him. She crawled up the stairs, almost dry heaving from the tears and screaming, trying to make it to her bed. She flung herself onto the bed and cried herself to sleep.

Her cell phone startled her awake. It was Andre. "I was calling to check on my baby and my baby's mama."

"Hi Andre." Andre could hear the dryness in her voice. "Whoa, what's up with you, baby girl?"

"Andre, you would not believe me if I told you. I don't even want to talk about it."

"What can be that bad? Come on, you can talk to me. I am the father of your child."

"Andre, stop."

"Okay, why don't you come over and I will call a masseuse and have them come out and give you a massage and hot rocks therapy."

"That sounds great, but no thanks; I have got some things I need to take care of." *Like killing Timothy.*

"Yolanda, come over and get your massage. Then you can relax and go home. I am not going to have my baby stressed out because of his momma. I hope to see you in an hour. Bye baby." Andre did not give Yolanda time to say no again. Yolanda got up and showered. She looked in the mirror. The bags and dark circles under her red eyes bothered her. She could use Visine to get the red out, but ice cubes would not even begin to touch under her eyes. She pulled out the Strivectin and dabbled a small amount under each eye. Yolanda headed to the closet, trying to find something cool to wear. She decided on a long, flowing white skirt and pairs it with a teal blue t-shirt and sandals.

She was starving by the time she arrived at Andre's and hoped that he had something good to eat. Being pregnant seemed to make you eternally hungry. He was already standing at the door when she arrived. He opened her door and helped himself to her, kissing and hugging her.

"Hey baby." Yolanda smiled and squirmed from his vice grip, and walked into the house. A spicy aroma hit her nose. "Something smells good."

"I did not have time to cook, so I ordered Thai. I know its one of your favorites."

"I am always down with Ty…" Yolanda winked at Andre and laughed at her play on words.

"The only person you better be down with is Andre Hunter." Andre tapped her on the bottom and kissed her on the cheek. He leaned down to talk to his baby.

"Hey little man, what's going on in there? This is your daddy, and I am going to be the best daddy in the world."

"Andre, you don't know that it's going to be a boy." "Yes I do. That's my son, Andre Hunter the second. He will be 'Dre for short."

"Oh, I'm glad you have decided on a name without consulting me." Yolanda smirked at him.

"What if it's a girl? What would her name be?" Yolanda dished a heap of basil fried rice on her plate.

"It's not going to be a girl, but if it was, I would name her Destiny."

"I'm glad you got it all figured out." After blessing the meal, Yolanda and Andre pigged out and retired to the living room. The masseuse was already waiting. The masseuse handed her a towel and introduced herself.

"Hi, I'm Crystal, and I will be taking care of you today. If you'll get changed, we will get started."

Yolanda loved the way the massage was relieving the tension in her neck. Timothy had gotten on her very last nerve, and she could not stop thinking about killing him.

"You are tense. I am going to have to work extra hard to get these kinks out." Yolanda did not even bother to answer. The hot rocks on her back felt so good. The heat seemed to penetrate down to her spine. Andre made sure that hot rock therapy was suitable for an expectant mother, and Crystal reassured him that it would be alright as long as the rocks were not too hot, and left on for an extended period of time.

Yolanda dozed off. When she woke up, Andre was stretched out on the couch watching a movie.

"What time is it?"

"Five o'clock."

"What? Why did you let me sleep so long? You know I have to get home and finish cooking for Timothy! Oh my God..." Yolanda almost fell off the table trying to get up so fast. Andre ran to her and helped her.

"Yolanda, you don't have to go home. You can stay here. Timothy can never hurt you again, not with me around. I would love him to start something with me. I will show him what it's like to get slapped around."

"Andre, calm down. You know that I just can't pick up and leave."

"Why not?" Yolanda could not answer the question. She just stared at Andre.

"I gotta go. Thanks for everything." Yolanda hugged Andre, and he kissed her deeply before she left.

The smell of the pot roast in the crock pot greeted Yolanda as she walked in the door. She was so glad that she had put it on this morning. All she needed to do was throw a few veggies and onions on top and cook some rice and dinner would be ready.

Death

CHAPTER 19

Yolanda arrived at the doctor's office ten minutes before her visit. She was so sleepy all the time, and found it more and more difficult to get up in the morning. She went through the normal routine of the pre-doctor work up and was waiting in the exam room. After what seemed like an eternity, her doctor finally came in.

"Hi Mrs. Clarke. How are you today?"

"I'm fine Dr. Wilkins. Thanks for asking."

"Alright let's see how you are progressing. Just lie back and relax and we'll get your measurements and listen to the baby's heartbeat." Yolanda lay quietly as the doctor went through her routine.

"Alright, you are right on schedule with a twelve week pregnancy. Everything looks fine and we will see you again in a month."

"Thanks, Dr. Wilkins." Yolanda breathed a sigh of relief, happy that her baby was fine. Now, her next task was to get some food in her stomach.

It was Friday evening, and Yolanda had packed the last of her personal items in her office. She was glad that the task that she had drug on for weeks was finally over. She put the last of the items in the box on her desk, grabbed her purse and headed down the hall to Timothy's office to ask him to carry the heavy boxes to her car. When she arrived, she saw Ms. Loleather coming out of the office with Timothy behind her. She tried to turn and walk away quickly, but they both saw her.

"Yolanda. I'd like to speak with you." Timothy wasn't smiling and Ms. Loleather just stared at her.

"I have a few errands to run. I was just coming to tell you. I will be back shortly."

"No, this cannot wait. I need to speak to you now. Wait in my office." Yolanda stood frozen. She knew that Ms. Loleather had told him about the pregnancy. Ms. Loleather walked past her, giving her the once over as she passed by. As soon as Ms. Loleather turned the corner, Yolanda turned to run, but Timothy was too fast. He grabbed her by the arm and swung her around to him. Yolanda yelled as he held her arm in a vice grip hold. She knew that Ms. Loleather had to hear her screams.

"Shut up!" Timothy slapped her so hard that she felt her teeth clink together.

"Get in my office, now!" Yolanda stumbled into his office, still dizzy from the ear-ringing slap. She fell into the nearest chair.

"Do you have some news that you would like to share with me?" Timothy sat on the desk in front of Yolanda, his face fiery red.

"Answer me!" Timothy punched Yolanda smack dead in the mouth, and blood splattered everywhere. Yolanda cried in pain, screaming, spitting blood.

"Timothy, what is wrong with you?! Please stop it!" Timothy walked over to the window and stood there staring out, saying nothing, rubbing his temples. She knew he would stand there at least five minutes, back turned, daring her to try to run away. That was just another way he controlled her; preying on her fear. Yolanda slowly slid her hand into her purse and grabbed her blackberry. She sent Andre a text.   911 church. Timothy was still looking out the window, silent. Yolanda looked at the door, wondering if she should try to make a run for it. She eased out of the chair, trying not to breathe, and bolted toward the door. She opened it and ran down the hallway, not even looking back, but hearing Timothy's footsteps behind her. She made it into the sanctuary.

"Deacon Thompson. Deacon Thompson." Yolanda ran to the altar. The altar that she had neglected so long. Timothy would not be crazy enough to keep beating her on the altar of the Lord.

"Deacon Thompson is not here, so don't waste your breath. I sent him to run a few errands. I made sure no one was here for this occasion. I had Deacon Thompson lock up the church. Ms. Loleather locked the last door on her way out. So, it's just me, you, and the Lord. "

Timothy's right palm connected violently again with Yolanda's cheek and she tumbled to the floor. Yolanda prayed that God would protect her baby and curled up in a fetal position, hoping that Timothy would not kick her. Timothy grabbed her by her hair, pulling her back to her feet.

"Take all of your clothes off." Yolanda cringed at the thought of being naked in the church.

"Timothy, surely you are not going to try to be intimate with me here. God knows…"

"Don't get it twisted, Yolanda. You are about to be baptized and delivered. You are carrying another man's child. You know the saying 'you lie down with dogs; you get up with fleas'. You've got fleas Yolanda, and you need a good cleansing." The look in Timothy's eyes told her that he was serious about whatever he was going to do to her. Yolanda realized that he had lost it. Yolanda could not deny the inevitable- Timothy intended to kill her. The thin sheen of perspiration on his head along with his clammy skin sent chills down Yolanda's spine. The next blow to her face sent more blood spattering down her chin and on her clothing. The scream that came from Yolanda's mouth seemed to make Timothy angrier as he yanked the buttons off of her suit and stripped her naked. The red-faced shame that filled Yolanda could have been seen a mile away- if there was anyone around.

"Timothy, why are you doing this to me? I have given you nothing but love, and this is what I get in return. I have given you every ounce of who I am, so much so that I don't even know who I am anymore. Between supporting you as the Pastor of this house and catering to your every need at home, my identity has been lost. And, this is how you thank me, having me stand naked and ashamed in God's house. Why?" The next blow sent Yolanda crumpling to the floor and she was quiet and still. Timothy was irate with her and she was helpless. Yolanda realized that she was suffering the consequences of an adulterous affair, but did God have to dish everything out in one day?

Timothy jerked her, picked her up and walked towards the baptismal pool. Yolanda remembered Timothy carrying her across the threshold of their hotel room when they were married. She recounted how happy she was to experience a dream come true that now turned out to be her worse nightmare.

CHAPTER 20

Andre nervously drove up the hill to BrightStar. He parked right on the curb in front of the church and killed the engine. He noticed Yolanda's car parked her reserved space. He opened the glove compartment and grabbed his blue-steel three-fifty seven magnum. He gripped the gun, hoping that Timothy would walk outside so that he could blow his brains out. Exasperated, he placed the gun back into the glove compartment. Even though Timothy probably deserved it, he could not bear to bring a gun into the Lord's house. Even though the shepherd had defiled it himself, Andre used better judgment. Instead, he grabbed his Louisville slugger that he always kept with him and ran toward the front door. He pulled the door, expecting it to open; surprised when it did not. Andre walked all around the church finding all of the doors locked. Finally, he grabbed a decorative stone from the landscaped grounds and threw it through one of the windows at the back of the church. He tried to kick the sharp edges off and climbed through, cutting himself despite his efforts. Andre eased his way inside, his ear listening for any sound. He heard faint talking as he quickly made his way down the hall toward the sanctuary. He hoped he would soon hear Yolanda's voice. If Timothy had harmed her or his baby in any way, there would be hell to pay. He kept moving swiftly toward the noises, being careful not to make a sound. This was the only time he was grateful for his past as a teen burglar. It helped him to be light on his feet, almost cat-like.

Timothy opened the door to the baptismal pool and shoved Yolanda inside.

"The Bible says in Mark the First Chapter and the fourth verse that John came preaching the baptism of repentance for the remission of sins. Now I baptize you in the name of the Father, in the name of the Son, and in the Name of the Holy Ghost. Get in the water, Yolanda."

"Timothy" Yolanda sobbed heavily, hoping for sympathy.

"I am standing here naked in the church. Don't you think you have humiliated me enough? I have already been baptized. I believe that Jesus is the Son of God. I believe that He rose from the dead. I believe He went to Hell and captured the keys of death. I believe that He now sits at the right hand of the Father. I believe that I have been baptized not only with water, but with the Holy Ghost fire. I have confessed my sins and iniquities before the Father, and he has forgiven me. So, there is no need for this. While it is certainly necessary, this water is only symbolic of cleansing and God has cleansed me all over again; I believe that from that bottom of my heart. He has made me whole and my faith is strong as ever. I know who holds tomorrow…"

Timothy grabbed Yolanda by her neck and picked her up off of the floor. Fear held Yolanda because she saw the look of evil and death in Timothy's eyes. There was urgency in him and Yolanda understood that this was the end for her. She prayed to God that he would receive her and her baby's spirit into heaven. She asked God to forgive Timothy for what he was about to do. The fear that she previously felt was now replaced by a peace; a peace that passed all understanding. She could no longer hear the angry words that Timothy spat at her anymore. As Timothy's clutch tightened around her neck, she felt the air unsuccessfully fighting to fill her lungs. Yolanda knew that it was futile to fight Timothy; she was not a match for his strength. She now realized what empowerment meant. It did not mean standing up to Timothy and his erratic and violent behavior; it meant being able to forgive him for everything he had done to her. That is what would give her the upper hand. Yolanda smiled and closed her eyes, no longer feeling the need to say anything else. She had received everything that she had asked God to do for her. Even though Timothy did not submit to the conviction that she knew God had placed on him, everything was alright now.

"What is so funny, Yolanda? You think this is a game? You better stop smiling and hope that Saint Peter lets you through those gates so that you can meet your Maker. This is the end of the road for you. Ashes to ashes and dust to dust."

"Timothy! Stop!" Andre stood inside the baptismal door brandishing the baseball bat, every nerve in his body standing on edge. Timothy loosened his grip on Yolanda and she dropped to the floor. Andre wanted to run to help Yolanda, but could not risk Timothy blind-siding him. He can see the deranged look in Timothy's eyes.

"So, you must be the dog. How'd you know where to find Yolanda? So, you are the reason that my wife is pregnant? Well, guess what, you can have her. Welcome to her funeral." Timothy smiled. A slight chill shook Andre.

"Look man, you don't have to kill her. She is just a victim of circumstance. I can help you; it doesn't have to end like this." Andre's eyes jetted back and forth from Timothy to Yolanda, watching for any movement.

"You help me? You are a nobody. I used to see you in the club carousing with your friends and Vicki. I know who you are 'Dre. So this is how you get back at me for taking your girl? You get my wife pregnant, and you want to help me? I am the Pastor of BrightStar Tabernacle. How can you help me?" Timothy chuckled at the thought of some lowly person who was so beneath him trying to offer him help.

"Look, man, I know what I was back then. Things have changed now; I am a different person. And this has nothing to do with Vicki. I would not try to repay evil for evil. Just let me take her and we will settle up."

"How cute. A strip club owner trying to quote scripture... I am not even trying to hear you man, so step off." Andre started toward Yolanda and stopped when he saw Timothy reach for his pocket. Timothy pulled out a taser and directed it towards Andre.

"You think you know the Bible, you don't know jack." Sweat poured down Timothy's face and he looked like a rabid dog.

"You thought you came to save the day, and now you're about to be a statistic."

"Timothy, think about what you are doing. How are you going to explain killing your wife inside your church? How are you going to explain why your wife is naked? What will your congregation think about this whole ordeal?" Timothy shuffled his feet and furrowed his brow. He used his free hand to wipe the sweat from his face, keeping his eye on Andre, hand on the trigger.

"I will tell them the truth. I'll tell everyone that you were having an affair with my wife. I'll tell them that we had a scuffle and I used the taser on you, incapacitating you, and Yolanda fell in the water and drowned. It's as simple as that."

"Timothy, she's naked. People are going to have questions. I can help you man. Just listen to me. You don't want to do this. I can get you the help you need."

Yolanda started to cough violently as she struggled to breathe after blacking out. Timothy kicked her in the ribs, sending her crashing into the wall. Andre's grip tightened on his bat and he ran forward swinging it at Timothy's head. Timothy squeezed the trigger on the taser as Andre charged him. Andre moved left quickly and one of the tasers' talons grazed his arm and flew past him. The bat made contact with Timothy's head and Andre cringed as he heard skull cracking and saw blood flowing. Timothy groaned loudly and fell backwards into the baptismal pool. Small orange sparks, puffs of smoke, and the smell of burning skin filled the air. Andre realized that Timothy was being electrocuted and tried to extend the bat to him to no avail. Andre could see the horror filling Timothy's eyes as the murky water enveloped him, his face frozen by the electric currents seizing his body. Andre looked away, unable to look death in the face. A few years ago, this would not have even fazed him. Andre heard Yolanda screeching loudly, terror overtaking her as she witnessed

Timothy's death, and ran to her to comfort her. He took his shirt off and placed it on her to cover her nakedness. Andre pulled out his phone and dialed 911. The white wife beater he was wearing did not do much to cover Yolanda's nakedness. Andre tried to console her as best he could.

Andre heard the police sirens and ambulances as they came up to hill towards the church. Yolanda was sobbing hysterically, looking at Timothy floating in the pool. Andre picked her up and carried her to the front pew and lay her down. The police used the rammer on the door and barged in and ordered everyone to put their hands in the air. Andre put his hands in the air and stood still, not moving a muscle. He knew the routine. The cops tackled him and handcuffed him without question.

"You have the right to remain silent…" Andre let the police go through their recitation without saying a word. He had been arrested enough in the past to know to just let them finish what they were doing, then answer their questions.

"What happened here today, son?" Andre looked at the lanky, red haired cop and started explaining the events to the cop.

"We got a floater up here; call in the Coroner's office." The muscular officer continued to peer into the baptismal pool behind the pulpit, watching Timothy float in a mixture of water and blood. The lanky cop looked at Andre with suspicion in his eyes, waiting on an answer. Andre recounted the events to the police officer, telling him how Timothy was going to kill Yolanda. "How do you two know each other?"

"I met Yolanda her a while ago and we became friends."

"What is the nature of your relationship?"

"Our relationship is platonic, sir." Andre could not bear to put Yolanda's name in the street and prayed his white lie would not catch up with him.

"Is everything that this gentleman stated true, ma'am'?" The cop directed his attention to Yolanda who was now whimpering softly. Andre hoped that Yolanda had taken in everything he said because he knew that the cops would interrogate them both separately.

"Yes, everything he said is true. My husband tried to kill me."

"You both will have to go down to the station for questioning. Why are you practically naked? Did he try to rape you or something?"

"No, he just told me to take my clothes off and he was going to baptize me." Yolanda tried to say as little as possible. The less they knew the better. The muscular officer returned with the clothes that Timothy had stripped from her. "Ma'am, do you need to go to the emergency room?"

"No officer, I will be fine, thank you."

"You look like you got beat up pretty bad. Are you sure you don't want to get checked out?"

"No, thanks." Yolanda could not risk going to the hospital and the emergency room personnel find out she was pregnant.

Yolanda and Andre sat in the back of the police cruiser waiting for the officer to take them to the precinct. Neither of them spoke. Yolanda looked back at the church and saw the paramedics loading Timothy's sheet-covered body into the ambulance. The coroner had arrived and was taking notes. Even though Timothy had tried to kill her, she still felt a loss. He was her childhood sweetheart and her husband. Yolanda still could not believe how he turned into a raging animal. On his worst day, Yolanda had never seen him so angry. Yolanda wondered why Ms. Loleather had to tell him. Yolanda pondered the question in her mind, knowing that she would probably never know the answer.

At the police station, Yolanda and Andre were separated and grilled extensively. Yolanda kept her answers as short and to the point as possible.

"Yes, there was a history of domestic violence." Another series of questions.

"I never filed a report because I was ashamed of the publicity it would bring to me and our church family"

"I refuse treatment because this is nothing new. I will just take a few Tylenol and I will be alright." Yolanda was so tired of answering questions. She could not wait to see her doctor tomorrow to make sure her baby was alright. She would never let "Red", who was standing in front of her with his arms crossed, know that she was with child. She could see the headlines.

THE SUNDAY MORNING WIFE

"Prominent Pastor Killed In Love Triangle."

By the time they were getting ready to leave the precinct, Yolanda's head was pounding. She instinctively reached for her purse to take some Tylenol, but realized she did not have it. "Excuse me officer, I don't have my purse." The red headed officer went into a small room and handed her the purse, without so much as looking at her.

"Thanks to you, too." Yolanda was already sick of the silent innuendos that the officers breathed. They acted like she wasn't even bloody and bleeding and looking like a hot mess. All they saw was Andre, rescuing a dame in trouble. The lover rescuing his forbidden love.

Andre called his friend Warren to pick them up, and also called a tow truck to tow his car to his home. There was no way he was going back to that church. A few people were already driving up as they were leaving, and he knew that the whole church was there by now. He wanted to shield Yolanda from as much of the bad publicity as possible.

CHAPTER 21

Yolanda's body screamed in pain as she exited Warren's car. Every nerve ending seemed to be on fire. She could not wait to get a bath and just lay down. Andre helped her to the house, almost carrying her. "I'm going to run you a nice, hot bath, get you some tea, and get you something to eat. Then we are going to call your doctor to see if she wants you to come in. We have to make sure that the baby is alright." Yolanda did not say a word. She hoped that the baby was fine. She could not believe that Timothy kicked her in the stomach, knowing that she was pregnant. It was his fault for having a vasectomy anyway. She squirmed as her hand brushed her busted lip. It was swollen, purple, and caked with dried blood. Yolanda was glad that Timothy could not harm her anymore, but she was still having a hard time believing that he was really dead. She started to cry again, visualizing him floating in the water. Andre held her tightly, caressing her hair.

"Baby, everything's gonna be alright. I am going to take care of you and my son. He cannot hurt you anymore. I know that it ended badly, but you are safe now."

Andre ran Yolanda's bath and bathed her. She was beaten so badly that he could hardly stand to look at her. Anger rose inside him once again, thinking of the many years of abuse that Yolanda had suffered at Timothy's hands. He gently washed the dried blood away from her face, and Yolanda winced every time he touched her.

"That hurts." Her whole face was starting to swell and her eyes were blackened and bruised. Andre prayed silently that the lack of oxygen from Timothy choking Yolanda had not harmed their baby.

Andre called the doctor on call and she told them to come to the maternity ward at the hospital immediately. Yolanda donned a robe and a pair of slippers.

"I need to go by the house to get some clothes. I cannot wear this to the hospital."

"Yolanda, I don't think anyone is going to care what you are wearing. It is not that serious. We need to get there as soon as possible. They want to put you on some kind of monitor to see if the baby's heartbeat is strong." Andre was nervous at the thought of possibly losing his child.

"Andre, it will only take a few minutes. I don't even have any underwear on. I am not going like this." Andre realized that it was futile to fight.

They headed out in Andres's Infiniti SUV. The tow truck operator had just arrived with the Lexus and was still unloading it. As they rode down highway 29, Yolanda was in a pensive mood. What is the BrightStar congregation going to think of me? I know Ms. Loleather will tell everyone about my pregnancy. They will think I meant to harm Timothy. I am going to be drug through the mud. Yolanda's phone ringing startled her from her thoughts.

"Honey, I just saw a breaking news report. They say Timothy is dead. Is that true?" Yolanda started crying again after hearing her mother's voice.

"Yes. It's true. Mom, it's a long story."

"I've got time." Yolanda let out a loud sigh and began recanting the events of the day. Her mother cried as she heard how her daughter was brutally beaten by Timothy. When they arrived at her home, Yolanda was still talking to her mother.

Cars had already lined up and down the sidewalk and people were standing in her front yard. She was thankful that Andre's car is tinted to the max and that no one could see her. They didn't bother to stop, and rode through the neighborhood, making their way to the hospital.

Yolanda's phone rang incessantly as made their way to the Maternity Ward. Andre was pushing her in the wheelchair like a maniac.

"Andre, slow down. You act like I'm in labor." She was tired of answering all of the calls. Everyone knew about Timothy. Some of the callers were sympathetic, and some were downright angry and threatening, calling her a killer. She turned her phone off; she was already drained, and could not bear to talk to anyone else. Yolanda did not want to sound morbid, but she was so glad that Timothy's parents were dead. Yolanda still remembered vividly the day they died in the tragic crash. They were hit by a tractor trailer on Interstate 85 that had jack knifed. They both died instantly. She could only imagine having to tell a parent that their child was dead. Timothy was an only child within a family that wasn't close-knit on either side, so she did not have to worry about calling too many people. Yolanda's thoughts drifted to her child and she rubbed her belly and said a silent prayer. She hoped that God would answer her, seeing how she had avoided Him so long.

They arrived at the nurse's station and Yolanda gave her insurance information to the nurse. She also told them to sign her in using an alias. She knew that everyone will be looking for her.

"Mrs. Clarke, I am Kiandra and I will be taking care of you. We have a room ready for you. Mr. Clarke, can you wheel her this way?" Neither Yolanda nor Andre bothered to correct the nurse. They both had one thing on their mind, and it was the well-being of their child.

"Sure. I'm right behind you."

Yolanda changed into the hospital gown and got into the hospital bed. The nurse strapped a wide band around her waist, put warm gel on her belly, stuffed a monitor underneath the belt and connected it to a machine. The nurse had explained all of the details of the fetal monitor, and Yolanda held her breath as the nurse made some final adjustments.

"Mrs. Clarke, I am just going to move this around until I find the baby." It was taking Kiandra too long to find her baby. Yolanda felt her palms becoming sweaty and she started to fidget.

"Mrs. Clarke, try to be still, please."

"I'm sorry, I'm just nervous."

"Ah, here we are." Yolanda loved the sound that she heard. It was her baby's heartbeat. She exhaled the breath she was holding forever and breathed deep, tears streaming down her face. She looked at Andre and he put his head in his lap, and breathed a sigh of relief, also. Kiandra made some adjustments on the monitor and wrote on the sheet that was printing from the instrument.

"Mrs. Clarke, the doctor will be in to examine you shortly." She left and Yolanda and Andre sat silently. Yolanda was so tired, and felt herself drifting off to sleep. Just as soon as visions of Timothy flashed across her mind, Yolanda was awakened by the doctor.

"Hi Yolanda, I'm Dr. Mims. I am just going to take a couple of measurements." She used a measuring tape to measure the length of Yolanda's belly. Then she examined the sheets of paper rolling off the machine.

"Everything seems to be alright. Your baby's heartbeat is strong and there is good fetal movement. The lab is on their way to draw some blood, and we will also get a urine specimen. We will observe you tonight and if everything is alright, we will discharge you in the morning. Now, would you like to address your injuries?" Dr. Mims automatically glanced at Andre.

"No, I would not. I am fine." Dr. Mims was not from the area and never had an opportunity to meet Timothy. Yolanda wondered if she would have thought he walked on water also.

"Tune in to the news and you will figure it all out."

CHAPTER 22

Yolanda was so glad that the maternity wing had its own private parking area. She did not want to run into any of the BrightStar parishioners. After being discharged from the hospital, Yolanda and Andre headed straight to McDonald's drive-through to get some breakfast. Yolanda longed to eat at the breakfast buffet at the Junction but knew it would be too crowded on a Saturday morning. Half of BrightStar would be there, eating the country cooking. After munching on a breakfast burrito and drinking a carton of milk, Yolanda reclined in the seat and closed her eyes. She felt totally drained and every bone, muscle and joint in her body ached.

Earlier that morning, Yolanda instructed the hospital to release Timothy's body to Johnson's Funeral Home in Greenville, South Carolina. She did not want to deal with any of the local funeral homes in Spartanburg. They all knew Timothy and she wanted to avoid any dirty looks from any of them. She already knew that the funeral will be a test for her. So, why not have some peace, if at all possible, before?

When they arrived at Andre's home, Yolanda climbed into bed. She was so exhausted; all of the events finally came crashing down upon her. She dreamed of Timothy, seeing him fall over and over into the baptismal pool with blood all around him. She could hear herself snoring, but was too tired to care. When she woke up it was seven o' clock in the evening. Yolanda could not believe that she slept that long, but understood that her body must have needed it. She looked around and saw Andre sitting in a chair nearby. "How long have you been here?"

"Just a few minutes. You did a lot of moaning, tossing and turning, so I just keep checking on you to make sure that you are okay."

"Thanks for everything. I don't think I could do this without you." Yolanda reached for Andre's hand and squeezed it firmly, holding it lightly against her bruised cheek.

"Well, there's a long road ahead, and we will take it one day at a time. I am here for the long haul, I ain't going no where." Andre climbed into the bed with Yolanda, and gently rested his head on her belly, so that he could talk to his baby.

Sunday morning rolled in and Yolanda felt funny not going to church. Considering the circumstances, BrightStar would only see her once again; for Timothy's funeral. Nevertheless, it seemed odd not having Timothy rush her to get ready. One thing that she surely would not miss was the violence.

Yolanda had removed the BrightStar tag from the front of her car, hoping to hide in some obscurity. She'd had enough of the harassing phone calls and had even gotten a new cell phone number. Her house had already been vandalized several times, from broken windows, small fires, to graffiti painted in her driveway. The gossip going around about her and Andre was relentless, and she had become an outcast.

Yolanda watched Pastor Jakes on TV as she ate the pancakes and turkey bacon that Andre prepared. She had already decided to take a nap after eating breakfast. She dreaded going to the funeral home to view Timothy's body. Part of her felt guilty for Timothy's death, yet, she had peace for the first time in years. How can I be happy that Timothy is dead? Yolanda prayed a silent prayer, asking God for his help. She also prayed for Timothy's family, and the BrightStar church family, despite the way she knew they were going to treat her.

CHAPTER 23

Yolanda looked at every store in the Northlake Mall, trying to find an appropriate suit for Timothy's funeral. She needed closure, and the funeral would certainly be final. Although she had gotten many death threats, she still had to go shopping. She hoped Charlotte was far enough away to get away from the BrightStar parishioners. She had on a toboggan, dark shades and a jogging suit, hoping no one would recognize her. Yolanda strolled into Macy's and was determined to find a suit there, whether or not she liked the style. She was tired and hungry, and could not wait to get her hands on a juicy burger with cheese, extra onions and pickles. Yolanda selected three black suits, and went to the dressing room to try them on. Satisfied with the third one, a Calvin Klein wool suit, she paid for it and left. The five hundred and fifty dollar price tag did not even faze her. She picked out a matching bag, shoes, and hat, and headed out; not even caring about the condescending look she received from the cashiers regarding her attire.

As Yolanda waited in the drive through for her food, she wondered how the church would act when she arrived at the funeral. She contemplated not going, but knew the congregation would have something to say about that also. She was darned if she did, and darned if she didn't. The whole ordeal was too much drama for one day and Yolanda tried to think of something else. She patted her tummy, and said hello to her baby.

Tuesday morning rolled around, and Yolanda sat in the car outside the mortuary, clutching the steering wheel, her stomach churning. The colorful fall leaves fell down on her car, like they didn't have a care in the world. Yolanda could not seem to make herself go inside. Another night of restless sleep, seeing Timothy die over and over again. She could only imagine what it would be like to see his lifeless body in the casket. "Yolanda, honey, you need to relax. This is not your fault. You are a victim in this whole situation." Yolanda looked over at her mother and smiled, silently thanking her for her reassurance. Yolanda glanced in her rearview mirror to look at her father's expression. He was blank, and she could not read him at all. She grabbed the charcoal gray cashmere Brioni suit and shoes that she purchased for Timothy. If he was not top notch, even in death, someone would have something to say.

Bob Johnson greeted them as they walked in the door of the funeral home. His hands were ice cold and Yolanda could feel the goose bumps spreading across her arms.

"Hello, and welcome to the Johnson Funeral Home. How may I be of service to you today?"

"I'm Yolanda Clarke, and I need to make arrangements for my husband Timothy Clarke. Late husband." Yolanda felt herself stammering and wanted to run out of the cold, stale room.

"Ah, yes, Mrs. Clarke. Please accept my deepest sympathy in the death of your husband. However, it is our duty to make this unfortunate experience bearable and as pleasant as possible. Let me assure you that we pride ourselves on taking excellent care of the deceased, and presenting them in as normal state as possible." Yolanda listened to his monotone voice and wondered how anyone could stand to be around dead people all day. She had to admire them, because the thought gave her the willys.

"Now, Mrs. Clarke, if you will follow me, let us prepare the funeral program." Yolanda and her parents followed Bob into another room that was lit brightly, and Yolanda was grateful. They perused the different types of programs available. Yolanda never imagined that so many types of paper, fonts and poems were available. Did she want a candlelight service? Did she want an open casket? What color and style of casket did she want? Did she have flower girls and pallbearers? Who would do the eulogy? Who would be singing? Yolanda jumped up and quickly exited the room crying. Why is planning a funeral so hard? Can he not see I am in no shape to even answer these questions? Yolanda looked in her purse and searched for her phone. She dialed the number and waited for an answer. "Deacon Elton Johnson, this is Yolanda Clarke... Yes, as good as I can be I guess.... I am trying to hold on as well as I can.....Yes, sir.... Deacon Johnson, could you come over to the Johnson Funeral home in Greenville and make these arrangements for me? Yes, sir... I want you to put the entire program together and spare no expense. I want everything top of the line... No, sir, you can handle everything.... I will be waiting for you... Bye...

Deacon Johnson finally arrived and gave Yolanda a long hug and a knowing look. Yolanda was grateful that someone knew the real Timothy, and could see through his farce. "How are you holding up, Mrs. Yolanda?" "I am holding on Deacon Johnson, just holding on, considering the circumstances..."

Yolanda sat quietly beside Deacon Johnson as he prepared the funeral program. He was on and off the phone, asking people to participate. No one turned him down, and once people found out he was handling the services, his phone started ringing; people were volunteering their services.

When the time came to view the body, Yolanda declined. She just could not seem to make her feet move in the direction they need to go. Seeing him at the funeral would be enough. She was already having nightmares, and decided against inviting more. Her parents and Deacon Johnson viewed the body. Yolanda let them know before they went that she did not want to hear anything about how he looked.

After dropping her parents off, Yolanda headed to Andre's house. Exhausted as usual, Yolanda planned to go directly to bed once she set foot in the house. Once inside, Andre greeted her with a kiss. She turned her head, feeling funny kissing him, after preparing her husband for burial.

"What's wrong honey?"

"Nothing, I'm just tired that's all. All of the preparation has drained me."

"Come sit on the couch; let me massage your feet."

"No, I am going to bed. I just want to be alone." Yolanda brushed past Andre, headed into the bedroom, and closed the door. The tears started falling before she could even get to the bed. Yolanda was so emotional from the pregnancy already, and the added weight of Timothy's death was almost unbearable. Plus, the guilt she carried felt like a ton of bricks. Yolanda cried in the pillow, hoping Andre could not hear her sobs.

Yolanda went to bathroom and looked at her face in the mirror. Her nose was Rudolph red. She wet a towel with cold water and held it on her face. Even though her eyes were swollen and red also, her nose just seemed to stand out. Yolanda hoped that the pregnancy would not make it swell too much more.

CHAPTER 24

The few family members that Timothy had left refused to ride with her in the family car. So, Yolanda, her mother and father were alone in a car that could have seated twice as many people. Yolanda struggled to walk down the aisle at BrightStar, feeling all eyes on her. Pastor William was reciting the twenty third Psalms as the organist played softly in the background. *The Lord is my Shepherd... I shall not want....*Somehow his cadence seemed to calm her, briefly. Yolanda could tell by the looks on some of the faces that they were not pleased with her being there. She felt that everyone was looking at her, and was glad the black hat and veil somewhat hid her on day a like today. Yolanda's feet seemed to feel heavier and heavier, like lead, as she approached the casket. She rubbed her palms together, feeling the thin sheen of perspiration covering them. Her heart was pounding so loudly that she could feel the beat in her ears, drowning out the whispers that she was trying to ignore. *Look at her....humph... She's got some nerve... Where is her boyfriend?*

Yolanda could see Timothy lying in the casket, and she swore the closer she got, he looked as if he was breathing. Yolanda was nervous now, thinking that Timothy was going to reach out and choke her again. She stopped dead in her tracks, afraid to move. Her father and mother, who were standing on either side, gave her a moment to regain her composure. Yolanda willed herself to move, and started taking baby steps once again. Out of the corner of her eye, she could see Ms. Loleather staring at her with a menacing glance. Her lips were sealed so tight that even a crowbar could not pry them apart. Her steely eyes were incapable of even shedding a tear…. Yolanda moved forward and saw Vicki crying quietly. Their eyes met for moment, and no feelings were exchanged; no sympathy, nothing. She was part of Yolanda's problem anyway. Yolanda saw Apostle Greene in the pulpit, looking at her with disdain. He was part of the problem too, telling Timothy to handle her in such an abusive way. He glared at her, and Yolanda glared back at him, until he finally looked away. She was already broken enough, and was not about to let him get under her skin.

She clutched the pacifier tightly in her sweat soaked hand, making her way slowly to the front of the church. Yolanda let the music from the organ soothe her, calming her nerves. Finally, she was standing in front of the casket, looking down at Timothy. She studied him hard, feeling the fear seep out of her body the longer she stood there. His normally bright skin looked like chalk paste. You're not so bad now are you? You can't touch me now… Yolanda stared at the place where the baseball bat cracked his skull, noticing the indentation and discoloration from the traumatic blow. Her stomach felt queasy as she recalled the sound of his skull splitting. Yolanda placed the pacifier on Timothy's chest and bent down to whisper in his ear.

"Does the baby want his pacifier?" Although Yolanda understood that he could not hear her, it gave her satisfaction to repeat one of his sarcastic comments. Yolanda was not happy that Timothy was dead, but she was happy that he could not hurt her anymore. She was finally free. She did not have to live in fear anymore.

Yolanda and her parents made their way to the front row, watching as Timothy's distant relatives said their goodbyes. None of them attempted to console her or even bother to look her way. She did not care. None of them knew what was like to live with an abusive person. They could have judged her until the end of time, but until they had walked in her shoes...

The service dragged on, and Yolanda did not know how much she could stand. Everyone was making Timothy out to be superhuman, and Yolanda wanted to scream. How could they have not seen through his charade? She knew that she could not blame them, because Timothy was a true chameleon, who changed his colors to acclimate to his environment.

As they finally prepared for the benediction, Ms. Loleather stood up. "I hope and pray that I ain't out of order, but I got somethin' to sey." Yolanda tensed as Ms. Loleather started to talk. Yolanda hoped that she would not tell everyone she was pregnant, but relaxed when she realized that no one knew that Timothy had a vasectomy.

"I'm sure ya'll saw Mrs. Yolanda put that pacifier in the casket. That's 'cause she is with child. She ain't tellin' nobody. I don't know why she keepin' it a secret. So, ya'll give her your best wishes and greet her on your way out." Yolanda felt l the heat rising in her face and glared at Ms. Loleather as she sat down and smiled triumphantly. Yolanda heard the strained silence, then whispers as she sat motionless, waiting for someone to say something. Pastor William finally spoke.

"If all hearts and minds are clear, let us dismiss. Father in the name of Jesus, we bow before you humble and sincere, thanking you for the life of our dear brother, Timothy..." Yolanda was still looking at Ms. Loleather, wondering what she hoped to gain by trying to expose her like that.

As they made their way to the cemetery, Yolanda clutched her parent's hands tightly. She could not wait till the whole ordeal was over and she could get as far away from BrightStar as possible. There was more talk graveside about how wonderful Timothy was and how he would be missed. Yolanda wanted to throw up. How could they not see him for the person he was?

It was finally over. Yolanda breathed a sigh of relief and started to walk directly to the car. She had to get away as quickly as possible and darted in and out thousands of people. Andre hired plain clothes security guards for her, against her wishes, and she was glad he did now after some of the comments she was hearing. Some of the people flat cursed her out. Right on the church grounds. The same people that were shouting, jumping, crying and praying on Sunday mornings were acting a straight fool. She guessed that was their Sunday morning face; just like she used to be the Sunday Morning Wife. When she was at church, Timothy showered her with love and affection. He made the church folk think that she was the best thing since sliced bread. He poured it on so heavy, that sometimes Yolanda almost believed him herself. But, before and after Sunday morning services, it was a whole different story. He treated her like the dirt under his feet. But, it was all over now. She could finally rest.

Yolanda wasn't about to go to the fellowship hall and eat. She knew it was time to head home. She had felt enough fiery darts to last a lifetime. Enough was enough. Vicki cornered her as she made her way to the car.

"Can I speak to you privately for a minute?"

"Vicki, I really need…"

"It will only take a minute." Yolanda reluctantly loosened her grip on her parent's hands and stepped away from them.

"What do you want Vicki?"

"Nothing really. I just wanted to congratulate you on your pregnancy. I'm sure that Andre is excited."

"Why would you assume that Andre is the father of my child?"

"Well, since I took Timothy to have his vasectomy, I am pretty sure that he cannot be the father." Yolanda's eyes widened in disbelief and she felt the urge to choke Vicki.

"And, I did catch you at Andre's house, remember? Don't worry, I won't tell anyone. You know, since Timothy's gone, I don't know how I'm going to make it. My little salary from the church can never keep up with the lifestyle I've become accustomed to, that's if they keep me on the staff. But, seeing the predicament we are both in, I am sure that we can work something out, can't we?"

"Well, seeing as how Timothy has almost depleted my inheritance keeping you up, there is nothing to work out. I will be starting from scratch rebuilding my life, and so will you. Instead of looking for someone to always keep you up, why not help yourself?

"Well, since I was employed as Timothy's secretary, I do know that the church gifted you both sizeable insurance polices. You will be getting that money soon." Yolanda did not even blink, ignoring Vicki's comment.

"Furthermore, if you think that little wind you just spilled from your sails is supposed to scare me, you still don't know who you're messing with. I am tired of being the tail, tired of being last, and I will not go down without a fight. I have been through too much to lie down and die now. I am in for the fight of my life, and if you think you want to contend with me; you better bring your A game. Now, I know there are warrants on you in several states. You would not want the police to receive an anonymous tip, would you? So, I think all of our business dealings are closed, don't you?" Yolanda pasted on a huge fake smile and patted Vicki on the shoulders, thanking her for coming to be a part of her husband's home going service. She walked off, glancing over her shoulders at Vicki, who was still standing there, with a blank look on her face. Yolanda figured the forty dollars she used to dig up facts about Vicki was well worth it. Yolanda smiled and waved at Vicki; laughing sarcastically at her as she rolled her eyes and continued to her car.

When Yolanda arrived at the car, Ms. Loleather was waiting on her. Standing beside her was Apostle Greene. "Mrs. Yolanda, we is so sorry for yo' loss. We hope you gon' be alright."

"I am going to be fine, Ms. Loleather. Now if you will excuse me." Yolanda tried to get in the car, but Ms. Loleather blocked her.

"Yo' beby gon' die. You a sinner and you gon' pay." Yolanda stooped down and looked her directly in the eyes.

"Oh, you mean the way you are probably paying for all of the innocent lives you took during your days as an abortionist?" Ms. Loleather's copper skin faded to a dull gray.

"Yes, I know all about it. I guess that's why you never had any children, huh? After all the ones you killed, God never let you carry one. That's why you are such a bitter woman! You were never able to have any! So many innocent lives you took, and you have the nerve to call me a sinner. What are you?" Ms. Loleather was silent; shocked that Yolanda knew her secret. Yolanda could see the wheels in her brain turning. Yolanda felt she was probably thinking-

"That was a long time ago, before Yolanda was even born; how could she have found out?" Yolanda looked at Apostle Greene, giving him the "you want some of this" look? He turned and quickly walked away, not saying a word. He was not going to give Yolanda the chance to expose him.

Yolanda sat in the car. Her breathing was labored, and she rubbed her hands together nervously. She was filled with so much anger that she trembled. She was so tired of church folks and how they acted like they had never sinned in their entire life. She felt that they acted like they were born saved and never ever messed up. It sickened her because the new people in church found that persona so hard to live up to. And when the new converts messed up, the church condemned them more than anyone, and told all their business. What ever happened to restoring one another in love? What happened to picking your brother and sister up? Tears streamed down Yolanda's face as she thought about the hurtful comments thrown at her today. How could Ms. Loleather say such an awful thing? Her baby was NOT going to die. Yolanda rubbed her belly and rebuked everything she said in the name of Jesus, and began to pray loudly, covering herself and her child in His blood.

CHAPTER 25

Yolanda arrived at Andre's house exhausted, and just wanted to lie down. She headed straight toward the bedroom.

"Yolanda, I know that you are tired, but you have to eat something first, then you can sleep all you want. If you want to talk, I'm here."

"Thanks, Andre, but I am too drained to talk. My head is pounding, and I need to rest." Andre cornered Yolanda and redirected her back to the kitchen. He prepared her a small bowl of pasta salad that he had prepared earlier. Yolanda wolfed it and went to the bedroom. She took her suit off, dumped it on the floor, and hopped in the bed in the spare bedroom. The day's adventures had taken its toll on Yolanda, and sleep was waiting for her around the corner.

Andre woke Yolanda the next morning.

"Wake up sleepy head breakfast is ready." Yolanda looked at the clock and could not believe that it was nine a.m. Where had time gone? Yolanda slowly rose and stretched, being careful not to hold her hands over her head too long. She had heard so much about getting the umbilical cord stuck around the baby's neck when reaching above your head. True or not, she did not even want to chance hurting her baby. Yolanda grabbed the robe from the edge of the bed, put it on and headed to the bathroom to freshen up.

As she entered the kitchen, she smelled the salmon cooking and her stomach turned a few loops. Salmon and grits were one of her favorites, but this morning, she could barely take the smell.

"Andre, could you please bring me a bowl of cereal to my room? I cannot take the smell of the fish this morning. And, light a candle, please."

"Yolanda, I'm sorry. I knew you loved salmon and grits and I thought I would surprise you. I guess certain smells and pregnancy don't mix, huh?"

Yolanda ran back to her room as she felt the tide rise in her stomach. She leaned over the commode ready to release, but only dry heaves came. She decided to take a quick shower after hugging the toilet. Who knew pregnancy could be so hard? Yolanda threw on a jogging suit after her shower and lay down on the bed. It seemed since she had become pregnant, that she could never get enough sleep.

Andre entered the room with a platter of cereal, hot tea, and orange juice. He placed the platter on the night stand and sat down on the bed next to Yolanda.

"Are you going to be alright? I can call the doctor and see if she could give you something for nausea."

"No, I'll be fine. I just need to rest. The past few days have taken its toll on me, I guess."

"Do you want to talk about it?" Andre hoped that she would say something about the funeral. He wanted to know how she was treated, although he surmised she wasn't received very well.

"Not one person even acknowledged me at the funeral. Not even Timothy's family. There were so many people that hurled insults at me that I was shocked. Even after the newspaper reports that Timothy was trying to kill me, and nearly succeeded, no one even spoke to me. I felt like the invisible woman." Yolanda broke down and began to sob.

"Timothy was my husband, and I did not want him to die. Even though he mistreated me, and I sometimes wished him dead, I really did not mean it. Even though he abused me mentally and physically, death is so- final. Now, everyone blames me for his death, like it's my fault." "Yolanda, don't worry, you know that Timothy's death is not your fault. He would have killed you, and if anyone is to take blame for his death it is me. But, I know that God has forgiven me, and that helps me out. I would do nothing different if I had to do it all again. I will protect you and my child at all costs, always remember that. Now, I know that it will take some time for you to grieve, just know that I am here for you." With that, Andre got up and left Yolanda to eat her breakfast. Yolanda ate, put the platter on the night stand, and went back to sleep.

Two months later, Yolanda was still eating and sleeping. She was halfway through her pregnancy and Andre had tried every way he could to lift her spirits. She didn't exercise or hardly move at all. She just slept all the time. He had even tried to get her involved in decorating the nursery, but she refused. She barely even left the house, and Andre was beginning to worry. He knew that it was futile to try to bring in a counselor because Yolanda would not open up to anyone that she did not trust. She refused to take the mild anti-depressant that the doctor had prescribed. Andre was at his wits end trying to help her and he was going to let her know it.

Yolanda was startled as Andre barged into her bedroom.

"Here you go Yolanda." Andre thrust her suitcases in her face.

"Here, just pack your bags, go somewhere and put yourself out of your misery. Nothing that I have tried to do for you has helped, so you might as well leave. You are just wasting away here in this bedroom day and night. You are not even getting enough exercise for the baby. If your life is that bad, and you don't think you have anything to live for, then leave." Andre thrust the suitcases in Yolanda's face once again. "I know that you have been through a great ordeal, but you can't just lie down and wait for death. God has blessed you with one of his greatest creations, and you are just going to lie around and die. He has dealt you a new hand, given you a new lease on life, and you just sit here. You asked God to deliver you from the abuse and he did. You asked him to protect your baby, and he did. Everything that you have asked him for, he has given you! But, I cannot remember the last time I saw you pray, read your Bible, or give thanks. I know that you are grieving, but you can't grieve forever. And stop agonizing over what Sister Loleather said about our child. He will not die. But, if you don't get up and dust the ashes off, neither one of you are going to live. If I can make it day after day, living with the guilt of killing someone, surely you can make it." Andre put the suitcases on the floor and put his head in Yolanda's lap and cried.

"What kind of compassionate and loving God would allow me to be abused for years? Don't talk to me about God, I will not listen. And I am not moving from this bed."

"Yolanda, I agree that you have been through a lot, more than the average person. But, remember Job in the Bible? I don't think that anyone suffered more than he did. But, he never lost his faith in God, and in the end, God restored to him more than he had in the beginning. Who would not serve a God like that? Remember, without a test, there is no testimony. Pass the test, Yolanda. God is a good God. When I look back and realize how many times he has saved me from death, I know that there is purpose for my life. He took a stealing, lying, cheating, low-down dirty stripper and turned him into a Witness. If God broke up the fallow ground of my heart, I know that he can heal yours. Don't shut God out and allow a root of bitterness to spring up. Yolanda, you and the baby are all I have. I cannot imagine living without you. I know that you are in a hard place right now, but Jesus has got you. Even now, his love for you is so great… just reach out to Him, cast your cares on Him, he is waiting for you." Andre stood up and walked out of the bedroom. He hoped that something he said would help her. The final decision would be hers. Andre just hoped she would choose life.

Yolanda lay in the bed and cried for hours. She prayed to God and asked His forgiveness for turning her back on Him. She got up, anointed herself and fell down on her knees and prayed, asking God to deliver her from the grip of depression.

Yolanda wailed and cried out unto the Lord, baring her soul before Him. Yolanda was determined to be free from bars of depression, and would stay on her knees as long as it took to be delivered.

Yolanda emerged from her room the next day sporting a black and teal jogging suit and black Reeboks. She was sporting a growing baby bump. Her hair was pulled back into a chignon and the glow of pregnancy filled her face. "Well, good morning, who are you?" Andre teased her as she pulled up to the bar to eat.

"Stop it, Andre." Yolanda smiled, and kissed Andre on the cheek, thanking him for jerking her back to reality.

"Cora, you looks good in that jogging suit this mornting." Yolanda laughed at Andre's made up line, making fun of one of Madea's plays. Andre loved all of Tyler Perry's plays and when he could fit a line in, he always did.

"Thanks, Mabel, now what's for breakfast?"

"A bowl of hot grits. You looking real hungry."

"Alright, Andre, stop playing. My name is not Al Green." They both laughed and dug in to a hearty breakfast of bacon, eggs, cheese grits and toast.

After breakfast, Yolanda wanted to walk to the lake behind his home and feed the ducks. He was so happy to see Yolanda happy that he did not care what they did, as long as it made her smile.

CHAPTER 26

Yolanda signed the last of the papers at the closing on the house that she and Timothy had shared. The house was already paid for and Yolanda was able to sell it at a profit. She had already packed up the house and auctioned off everything inside to charity, except the family heirlooms. Yolanda did not want to remember anything about the life she shared with Timothy.

She thought about the last time she walked through the house. Each room had its own private story to tell. No one would ever know the physical, emotional, and mental torture she endured. Like the time he tied her to the dining room chair for twenty four hours because she was late for church. Or, the time he made her stand on one leg in the corner of the den for one hour. All because he thought she had opened his mail. How could she forget the times he made her spend the night in the garage on cold winter nights without so much as a blanket or a sleeping bag? He made sure she could not get into either car. The only warmth she had was the clothing she was wearing at the time. She exercised on and off those nights, not breaking a sweat, moving just long enough just to stay warm. Yolanda did not even want to think about the time he locked her in the crawl space under the house because she did not call before going to the mall after work one day. He swore she was meeting some other man.

But this was a new day, and Yolanda had forgiven him for the verbal, physical, and mental abuse, and the attempt he made at killing her. It was now time to move on.

Yolanda realized that she could not keep living with Andre. Even though they both had rededicated their lives to the Lord, the temptation of being intimate while living together was too great. Yolanda was thankful for the insurance policy that the church had purchased, knowing the money would help her find a small place for herself and the baby. Of course, they tried to nullify her policy after some people in the church circulated a rumor that Yolanda and Andre planned to kill Timothy. Even though the police told them that Andre killed Timothy in self-defense, they chose to believe otherwise. Timothy was bigger than life to them, and they refused to believe that he would try to kill someone. Although Ms. Loleather made sure that everyone knew that Yolanda was pregnant, they would never know for sure that the baby was Andre's. Timothy took the secret of his vasectomy to his grave, just as he wished.

CHAPTER 27

It was the coldest winter night Yolanda had remembered in while. The early December air seemed to bite her as she walked towards Target to pick up a few extra items for the baby. She was now thirty six weeks pregnant, and time was running out. It wouldn't be too much longer before she could hold her newborn baby. She thought about what Ms. Loleather said, and quickly cast her mean-spirited words down.

The Christmas music blared above her head and Yolanda sang along. "Have a holly jolly Christmas…" Everyone was scurrying about, trying to prepare for the upcoming holidays. Yolanda was looking for sleepers for her baby when she felt liquid running down her legs. Soon after, a gush came, and Yolanda realized that her water had broken. Workers from all over the store went into panic mode, trying to figure out who should call an ambulance. Yolanda calmly used her cell phone to call 911 and then called Andre and told him to meet her at the hospital. She then went over to the Home and Garden center and stretched out on a chaise lounge. THEN THE PAIN CAME. Yolanda doubled over as the first contraction hit her like a truck. Throughout all the birthing classes that she and Andre took the instructors told her that she would be able to distinguish a Braxton-Hicks contraction from the real thing, and they weren't lying.

When she arrived at the hospital the nurse took her straight up to her birthing room and started to prepare for a new baby. Andre walked in like a nervous cat unable to be still.

"Yolanda, are you alright? Do you need anything? What can I get for you?"

"Andre, calm down, the nurses have everything taken care of and I am…" Yolanda gripped the rail on the bed as the pain ripped through her body. She now knew what her mom must have gone through to give birth to her. Yolanda had called her parents in the ambulance and they were now on their way. After much prepping and labs being drawn, the Doctor said that it was alright for her to have an epidural. Several hours later a much more relaxed Yolanda pushed a beautiful seven pound nine-ounce baby boy into the world. The nurse laid the baby boy on her chest and Yolanda smiled.

"Hey, my little man." Andre beamed as he looked at his son. "I told you it would be a boy." Yolanda rubbed and kissed her baby's forehead, and he looked her intently, like he knew who she was.

"You know your mommy's voice, don't you Donovan Isaiah?"

"What happened to Andre?" Andre lightly stroked his son's cheek.

"He looks like a Donovan."

"I don't care what we call him, he is my son." Andre bent down to kiss Yolanda and his seed on their foreheads.

Yolanda picked up the baby carrier and peeked under the blanket to see if Donovan was still sleeping. Her parent's did not care if he was still asleep or not, they were determined to hold him. Yolanda's life had changed completely since he was born six weeks ago. Donovan was a beautiful round baby with chocolate skin and gorgeous dimples and huge brown eyes, just like his dad. Yolanda thought that he was perfect in every way. The labor was intense and painful; lasting eight whole hours, but the end result was worth it. Yolanda reminded herself that eight meant new beginnings, and every pang of labor was worth it.

Yolanda spent the day at her parent's house, watching them dote over Donovan. He was growing so fast and squirmed as her parent's planted kisses all over him. She finally told them that Andre was the father, glad she did not have to keep secrets any longer. Every time Yolanda looked at Donovan, she prayed that God would protect him and let him grow old. Ms. Loleather's words about the Lord taking Bathsheba's child still haunted her sometimes.

"Yolanda, are you okay?" Her mom was looking at her worriedly. "I'm fine mom, just thinking, that's all." Yolanda leaned over and kissed Donovan.

"Hey, my little fat man." She kissed him some more, finding it hard to believe that she could love someone so much.

"Mom, we need to get back home."

"No, don't take my baby. It took me a long time to become a grandma." Yolanda's mother took Donovan from her arms and held him to her breast.

"You are grandma's baby aren't you? Tell your mommy to leave you with me." Yolanda's dad peeked from behind the newspaper he was reading.

"Honey, give that baby back to Yolanda. We can't coddle him so much. We have to make him a strong man, so his Papa can take him fishing." Yolanda looked at her dad's smile. He seemed so happy to finally be a grandfather.

Andre must've heard the car because he was already coming out of the garage door smiling.

"How's my son?" Andre opened the door and picked Donovan up out of the car seat, his large hands swallowing him. "Hello to you too, Andre."

"Do I detect a hint of jealousy, Yolanda?"

"Whatever." Yolanda smiled and grabbed Donovan's diaper bag and followed Andre into the house. She was grateful that Andre had stood by her during her pregnancy. He was there in the delivery room the whole time; he never left her side. Even before he was born, Andre had asked Yolanda to marry him so that their child would not be born out of wedlock. Andre did not want to give anyone a chance to call his son a bastard, like he was called so many times as a child.

Andre played with Donovan, then gave him a bottle. After Donovan fell asleep, Andre put him in his crib in the nursery and came back and sat down with Yolanda on the couch.

Yolanda felt that it was time for "the speech", and prepared herself.

"Yolanda, we should get married. Donovan needs a full-time father. I can't stand the thought being separated from either one of you. The thought of you moving out is too much. You know that I love you both more than life itself, and I am committed."

"Andre I am not ready for marriage. It has only been a few months since Timothy's death, and I am still finding myself. I have to know who I am before I commit to anyone. And what will people say?"

"I don't care what they say. We are not bound to South Carolina. We can always move."

Later on that night, Donovan startled her with a loud piercing scream. Yolanda had never heard that type of cry from him before and immediately knew that something was wrong. She ran to his crib, reached down and patted his head to comfort him. When she touched his head, he was burning up. Yolanda has never had a child, but instinct told her his fever was dangerously high. How could he have gotten sick so fast? Andre always joked with Yolanda saying she was "germophobic" as far as Donovan was concerned, because she always took extra precautions regarding his well being after what Ms. Loleather said. "Yo' baby gon' die…" echoed over and over in Yolanda's head.

"I rebuke you Satan in the name of Jesus! My child shall live and not die!

"Andre, get us to the hospital, fast!" Yolanda was frantic, and Andre can tell by the look in her eyes that it was serious.

Donovan's screams had quieted to an eerily soft moan, and Yolanda was concerned.

"Andre, please hurry." Yolanda fought back tears and prayed in the Spirit because she could not even find words in English.

Andre pulled up to the emergency ramp at Spartanburg Regional, jumped out and opened the door for Yolanda. Yolanda was carrying a now limp Donovan in her arms as they both scurried to the Triage area.

"Help! Someone help! My son is sick!" Yolanda was hysterical and crying loudly.

"What's wrong with him?" one of the Triage nurses inquired.

"I don't know. He was asleep in his crib and he screamed, I touched him and he was burning up. Now, he's just gone limp." Yolanda was breathing heavily and feeling faint. The nurse has already grabbed Donovan and was taking him back to an examination room as Yolanda was talking. Yolanda grabbed Andre's shoulder to steady herself as her legs became unsteady.

"We got a mother going down out here..." was the last words that Yolanda remembered.

Later on that evening after he was transferred, Yolanda stepped in the Pediatric Intensive Care Unit at Greenville Memorial Hospital and saw all of the tubes and IV's in Donovan. Her parents had arrived at the hospital after Andre alerted them to the emergency. Tears were streaming down her cheeks and she would trade places with Donovan in a heartbeat if she could. No child should have to go through this. Yolanda wished that he could talk so that she could ask him if he was in pain. She wanted him to open his eyes so that she could at least look into them to see how he was feeling. Andre stood beside her and held her hand as they both choked back tears. They were waiting on the test results of a spinal tap to come back, which they performed because Dr. Newton said his white count was very elevated. Andre and Yolanda hugged each other and kissed Donovan on the forehead.

The doctor came in and the solemn look on his face tells Andre and Yolanda the news is not good. "We've got the test results back from his tap and it looks like he's contracted bacterial meningitis of some form. The high fever of one hundred four point five, malaise, and his elevated white count at twenty-two thousand sent us in the direction to do the tap. The bad thing about this type of meningitis is that it can cause swelling in his brain, seizures, and even death. I will be up front with you both. He is a very sick little baby, much younger at six weeks old than what we are used to seeing. It will take a miracle to save his life. If he does live, he may have brain damage, hearing loss, and severe learning disabilities." Yolanda dropped to the floor upon hearing the news. She sobbed and cried, pounding the floor with her hands.

"No, No, No! My child will live! He will be fine! He will not have any disabilities!"

"Mrs. Hunter, I am just her to state the facts. I have to be upfront with you, but I promise you that we will do everything within our power to save your son."

"I appreciate that Dr. Newton, but I am going to go with God on this one. I have to rely on His power. I thank you for everything you and your staff have done for Donovan, and I pray that God will give you insight and wisdom as how to care for my son. Thank you so much. I am sorry that I'm so emotional, but I have waited years and years to have a child, and I cannot lose him like this. I just can't."

"We will continue to update you on any new information regarding your son as we get it. Thank you." Dr. Newton walked out and Yolanda leaned against Andre and braced herself.

Yolanda knew that this meant war. She understood that the battle would not be hers, but the Lord's. She put on her warrior face and was prepared to fast and pray until she took Donovan home with her. She grabbed her oil out of her purse and anointed herself, Andre, and Donovan. She asked Andre to lead them in prayer as they touched and agreed on Donovan's healing.

After a powerful prayer, Yolanda walked toward the door. "I'm going to the chapel at the hospital."

"Do you want me to go with you?"

"No, I don't ever want Donovan to be alone. I want him to be able to hear at least one of our voices at all times." Yolanda walked down the corridor of the hospital and looked for directions to the chapel. All of the corridors looked alike; the same eggshell walls and shiny linoleum floors. She finally located the chapel, and walked in. It was a small room with candles and a small altar. Yolanda flung herself on the altar and began to pray, weep and wail. She quoted every scripture that she could think of and told God who He was and who she was in Him.

"O God, my King and my Lord, I beseech you God, asking you to have mercy upon my son, Donovan. My God, you sent your Son Jesus that we might have life, and have it more abundantly. I call upon your angels, Master, that they will dip down in your healing waters and come and touch my son now, in the name of Jesus." Yolanda disregarded the mucus that was running from her nose. She didn't care about her personal appearance at such a critical time. She used her sleeve to wipe her nose and kept praying.

"You are Jehovah -Jireh, my Provider, You are Jehovah - Shalom, my Prince of Peace, You are Jehovah-Rophe, our Healer, You are Jehovah-Shammah, You Are Here! You are the MESSIAH, THE LORD GOD ALMIGHTY, THE GREAT I AM! I invoke your presence God; I lift high and magnify your Holy Name. You alone are God and there is none like you. I thank you for Donovan's healing because your word says to "speak those things that be not as though they were". I call forth complete healing in the name of JESUS, I stand on your word O God, faithful that you will do it."

"Yolanda." Yolanda turned when she heard her name. It was her mother. "Andre wanted me to come and get you; the doctors want to have a conference with the family.

"What time is it, mom?"

"It is seven o'clock in the morning. You have been praying all night long."

Yolanda and her mother walked down the corridor back to Donovan's room. Dr. Newton and another Pediatric Neurosurgeon were there waiting. Dr. Newton spoke first.

"Donovan's condition has deteriorated rapidly. While we have isolated the bacteria that has caused the meningitis, a Neisseria strain, and started antibiotics, his brain is severely swollen. I called in Dr. Narabai, who is a Pediatric Neurosurgeon, to see if surgery would help relieve the swelling. We scanned him first, to see how much brain activity there was, and found it to be minimal. I am sorry. As, you can see, we are preparing to put him on a respirator, which will breathe for him. We will leave you all now to make a decision on when to pull the plug on his respirator."

PAMELA D. RICE

The doctors walked out and left Yolanda and her family wide-eyed and glued like cement to the floor. Yolanda heard soft whimpers coming from her parents and turned to Andre. She could see the floodgates in his eyes that were about to break, and the dam opened on her eyes as well.

"I cannot accept this. I know God heard and answered our prayers. I know he did." Yolanda and Andre cried and held each other tightly. Yolanda wanted so badly to wake up from the nightmare and go back to her happy world. Yolanda's mother brushed her hair out of her red, swollen eyes.

"Honey, I don't understand, but I will keep praying, and if Donovan doesn't make it, what better consolation can we have than knowing that he is with the Father?"

"No, he will not die. I asked God to keep him and heal him, if I give up now, I will not be standing by what I prayed for. Where will my faith lie, in what the doctors said, or what God says in his word? I am going to trust God, and take him at His Word. He said that he is not a man that he should lie, nor the Son of man that he should repent, and what He has blessed is blessed! I know that he said the fruit of my womb would be blessed, and I am holding Him to his word! If there is any doubt in anyone's mind that Donovan could not be healed, please leave now. But, if you know God, and know that He is a burden- bearer, a heavy- load carrier, then please stay and pray with us. Our son will be resurrected by the morning light.

Rebirth

CHAPTER 28

Yolanda and Andre prayed all night long, asking God to heal Donovan. Andre broke the curses that Ms. Loleather spoke over Donovan and sent them back to the pits of Hell. They prayed in the Holy Ghost when they could find no more words. Yolanda lay before the Lord like a woman in travail. They both cried and pleaded with the Lord to save Donovan's life. Yolanda knew that if God wanted to truly show His power and might, and show Himself to her, today would have to be the day. She knew that she would not be able to live without Donovan, because he had brought so much joy to her life. Yolanda never thought she could love anyone as much as she loved her son. Just being able to finally see him after carrying him for almost nine whole months was sheer joy. She remembered laying awake at night wondering what he would look like, would he love her, would he be a good baby, would he be normal?

Dr. Newton stepped into the room.

"Good morning. We need to try and wean Donovan off of the life support. If he is able to sustain breathing on his own, then he will have a chance. I am not going to give you two any false hope. I stated in the beginning that it would take a miracle to save his life. We will wean him slowly off the support system, hoping that he will breathe own his own."

"He's going to live, Dr. Newton." Yolanda couldn't bring herself to give up on Donovan, or God.

Yolanda smoothed her unkempt hair back and rubbed the dark circles her eyes had become.

"Mrs. Hunter, there is no way in this world that your son is going to live. I have tried to be as frank as I possibly could be with you. I know what your expectations are. The nurses have heard you both praying all night, and that is good. But, let's face reality here. Look at your son. He has not responded to anything or anyone. There is nothing left there, except his little body."

"You're wrong Dr. Newton, he is alive." Yolanda walked to the bedside and watched Andre stroke Donovan's cheek.

"Donovan, I know you hear me, you will live and not die! All of the promises of God are Yea and Amen, and this is your promise, that you will live." Yolanda bent down and gently kissed Donovan on his forehead. She looked at Dr. Newton as he threw his hands up in exasperation and walked out.

The respiratory therapist began to turn down the oxygen levels on the machine that maintained Donovan's life. All of the nurses, doctors, lab staff, secretaries, and anyone else affiliated with Donovan's care came by to say goodbye. Their teary eyes told the story of attachment that comes along with hoping the little ones make it.

Yolanda and Andre ignored their farewell wishes and held strong to the belief that God would raise their son. Out of gratitude, they allowed everyone to say their goodbyes, not once giving in to the notion that Donovan would die.

At twenty percent oxygen, Donovan began to cough and sputter violently, his lungs searching for the air that had helped him breathe. Yolanda calmly talked to Donovan.

"Just relax sweetheart. Everything is gonna be alright." Yolanda started to sing his favorite lullaby, hoping that it would calm him enough so that he could get his breathing together.

"Rock- a -bye baby, in the treetop, when the wind blows, the cradle will rock." Donovan relaxed and became still, and

Yolanda saw his eyes flutter as he tried to open them. His tiny hands curled around each of his parents' fingers they had placed inside his tiny hand. Donovan took one deep breath; then silence. Several nurses began leaving the room, tears streaming down their faces.

"Everyone please stop crying, he's not dead. He's just being refilled." "Mrs. Hunter, let's be real..."

"No. Get out, everybody out!" No one moved.

Yolanda leaned over the bed and cradled Donovan in her arms. Come on God, you've worked greater miracles than this. Lord, I know you said the fruit of my womb would be blessed. Show yourself Lord. My Lord, My GOD, show yourself this day! Tears gushed down Yolanda's and Andre's cheeks as they cuddled Donovan together. The river of tears that Yolanda was crying flowed down onto Donovan's forehead and trickled into his eyes, nose and mouth. Donovan inhaled sharply and sneezed. He gagged and sputtered and let out the most shrill, high-pitched scream that Yolanda and Andre had ever heard in their life. He began to cry, and Yolanda ran around the room, almost knocking Donovan's IV pole down to the ground. Andre steadied the pole and Yolanda. The staff stood in disbelief, dumb-founded by the miracle that had taken place. Dr. Newton ran back into the room upon hearing Andre's and Yolanda's screams, sure the baby was dead.

"Oh, my God! He's alive! Quick, start protocol two for infants! Get him back on oxygen, nasal. Hurry!" The staff stepped into action, quickly stabilizing Donovan.

Andre and Yolanda fell to the floor. They hugged each other and cried aloud unto the Lord. They would never forget the miracle that God performed.

Yolanda watched as the staff took care of Donovan, and wiped the tears from her eyes. Only God could have saved him, and He did. Yolanda was drained, but jubilant. Dr. Newton stated that he wants to watch Donovan for at least another week, and perform some more diagnostic tests to make sure that there was no brain damage. If everything was alright, Donovan would be released.

Seven days later, they were on their way to Andre's home, with a fully recovered, miraculously healed Donovan in tow.

Yolanda could hardly stand to let her baby out of her sight. She often found herself standing over his crib, making sure she could see his little chest rising and falling.

CHAPTER 29

Yolanda stepped on the porch of her Atlanta home to water her leafy ferns and bulging pink begonias. She had gone flower crazy since moving, (a new hobby to keep her mind occupied). Yolanda had developed a quick green thumb and spent countless hours in the library researching flowers indigenous to her surroundings. She had also taken some horticulture classes at the local Community College. She had never felt so much peace in her life before. All of the nightmares HAD FINALLY CEASED. Seeing Timothy lying in the baptismal pool bleeding and electrocuted left a vivid picture imprinted on Yolanda's brain that she thought she would never stop seeing; a movie still being replayed over and over again. Yolanda finally appreciated the fact that with God all things are possible; she now realized what that meant. If it hadn't been for Him, she knew that she would have lost her mind. With all of the tragedies she had endured Tara, Timothy, and almost Donovan; she hoped God realized that she had longsuffering down pat! Yolanda smiled, wondering if God thought her sense of humor was funny.

Yolanda heard Donovan crying and ran back inside to check on him. He was peeking between the rails, knowing his mommy would be there very soon. Yolanda picked him up and planted kisses all over his soft body. "Are you hungry?" She went into the brightly lit kitchen and fed him and then gave him his sippy cup. After Donovan finished his milk, Yolanda changed his diaper. Yolanda could not believe that someone so little could go to the bathroom so much. But, she did not mind. She was just glad he was alive. She played and sang to him, and when he became fidgety, she rocked him to sleep.

"Rock-a-bye baby, in the tree top." Donovan was asleep in no time, and Yolanda smiled as she placed Donovan down for his nap. She stood there for what seemed an eternity staring at him, thanking God for him, and asking God to keep him safe from all hurt, harm and danger.

Yolanda sat down in the rocker in Donovan's room and took a moment to think about her upcoming wedding. She glanced down at the three carat ring Andre had given her and beamed. Yolanda had already picked out an ivory Vera Wang contemporary wedding dress, and she had worked out daily to lose the seventy extra pounds she had gained during pregnancy. Yolanda was certain that Andre had to love her, because even when she was heavy, he never said anything negative to her about her body or weight. Yolanda made a mental note to call Sharon. She was on the Management staff at Cator Woolford Gardens at the Frazier Center in Atlanta, where the small intimate wedding ceremony would be held. The wedding guest list included her parents, Andre's old friend Warren, and Reverend Thompson. Reverend Thompson was Andre's childhood neighborhood preacher. He had tried many times to get Andre to walk the straight and narrow when he was younger, but Andre never listened. When Donovan became sick, he was the only person Andre knew to call, and he was still right there at Philadelphia Baptist Church in Atlanta, after all those years. Since then, Andre had been under his wing, learning all he could. There would be no best man or maid of honor; they had each other and their son. The first time Yolanda walked on the premises and into the gardens, she knew that this would be the place that she said "I Do." Yolanda made another mental note to call Lois at G&M Events. Yolanda let them plan everything, from the stationary down to the small intimate dinner they would have. Yolanda figured she did not need the stress and worries of having to plan a wedding, and decided to let someone else handle it. They would present and idea, and if she liked it, she accepted. If not, they went back to the drawing board.

The door bell rang, and Yolanda was jarred from her private thoughts. She went to the door and looked into the peephole.

"Hello, Mrs. Hunter, how are my favorite people doing today?"

"We are fine, Andre. What brings you by so early?"

"I came to whip up some breakfast for my wife, then run a nice bath for her, then take her into the bedroom and make passionate love to her for hours."

"Andre, you know we have both talked about this. We will not be intimate with one another until after the wedding. We have gone through so much, and I don't want anything to ruin our future together. All of the drama that stemmed from our adulterous relationship is in the past, and that's where I want to keep it. I want God to be pleased with everything we do. But, don't think for one minute this is easy. You make a sister want to get her groove on in a bad way." Yolanda smiled and kissed Andre lightly on the mouth.

"How bad?"

"Andre, stop before we get into trouble. What did you have in mind for breakfast?"

"Well, since you ruined the moment, why don't we just go to IHOP for breakfast?"

"No, I just put Donovan down for his nap, and I don't want to wake him. How about I plug the waffle maker up and make some waffles? I got some leftover chicken in the fridge that I can warm in the oven, too."

"Chicken and waffles sounds good, but I had waffles yesterday. How about chicken and grits instead?"

"Chicken and grits it is."

After eating, Andre drove to the church to meet Reverend Thompson. He had relayed to Yolanda about how they had been going out into the community to reach the gang bangers, pimps, homeless, prostitutes, and anyone else who would listen. Andre thought it ironic that the very man he used to curse daily was standing beside him witnessing the Gospel of Jesus Christ. Andre knew that Reverend Thompson was a true man of God, being able to forgive him of all of the foul and vulgar things that he said to him. After a long day on the street, Andre and Reverend Thompson head to his home. Andre relayed that he was disappointed that they hadn't had one person receive Christ, thinking their mission had been unfruitful. "Son, anytime you witness to anyone, it is never unfruitful. One plants, another waters, but it is God who makes the increase. Just keep planting seeds son, keep planting seeds."

Andre and Reverend Thompson spent the rest of the evening in Bible Study. Andre always talked about how much he had learned from Reverend Thompson. He always said he felt like he had an example of what holiness was. Even though Andre knew he was far from what God wanted him to be, he was thankful that he wasn't what he used to be.

CHAPTER 30

Yolanda sat at the dressing table trying to decide which lip gloss to wear. She could not believe that her wedding day had finally arrived. Yolanda settled on the MAC Pale Pink Lip Glass and put the finishing touches on her makeup. Yolanda's mother sat patiently beside her, keeping an eye on Donovan. He was entering his terrible two's and into everything that he could get his hands on. Yolanda wondered what Andre was doing and decided to give him a call on his cell.

"Just calling to make sure you hadn't tried to skip town."

"Are you kidding? Nothing can keep me away from you this day. This is going to be one of the best days of my life."

"I love you Andre."

"I love you too Yolanda."

Yolanda slid into her Vera Wang gown. It was a soft strapless mermaid gown with full-length rouching details in off white. Yolanda had worked hard to get her figure back, working out with a personal trainer three times a week, and the sweat had finally paid off. The gown hugged every curve on her body, and Yolanda loved it. She looked at herself in the mirror and hoped that Andre would be pleased. She loved the person looking back at her in the mirror. Her life had come full circle. She had gone from trying to make sure everyone else was happy, even if it was at her own expense, to making sure she was happy first. Not that she was being selfish or narcissistic, but realizing that she could not help anyone with any of their problems in life until she had her own life under control. Yolanda's mother helped her put on the diamond micro pave pearl necklace and matching earrings and stepped back to admire her daughter.

"You have to be the most beautiful bride that I have ever seen. Yolanda, I know that we probably haven't been the best examples of parents that a girl could have, but I want you to know that our love for you has never dwindled. I just want you to know that we will never lose sight of what's important again in life. There is nothing in the world that's worth sacrificing your family for, your father and I understand that now. We prayed to all of the gods when you were going through with Timothy's death, and only Jesus answered our prayers. That's when we realized that we had only been chasing foolishness, and not our destiny. We quickly rededicated our lives to Christ, and well, you know the rest." Yolanda's father tapped on the door, signaling that it was time to go. Yolanda grabbed the bouquet that the G & M event staff had left for her. Yolanda was pleasantly surprised. The staff had chosen a beautiful ivory calla lily bouquet accented with maiden hair fern, olive branches, and miniature ivy, all tied with a beautiful satin ribbon. Yolanda's mother adjusted her veil that was also accented with small flowers and makes sure her upswept hairdo was in place.

Yolanda's mother picked Donovan up and hurried to take her seat. Yolanda and her father stood at the entryway into the garden, waiting on the music to start.

"You look absolutely beautiful Yolanda. I am prouder than any father can be at this moment. I wish you, Andre and Donovan a lifetime of happiness. You certainly deserve it. I'm sorry for not being a part of your life, but this is new season…"

"Dad, stop, you are going to make me cry." The music started and Yolanda slowly moved down the aisle to a new life.

Andre tried to catch his breath when he saw Yolanda coming towards him. She was stunning, and Andre realized all that they had been through was worth this moment in time. A solitary tear rolled down Andre's cheek as he reached for Yolanda's hand. Reverend Thompson performed a short and sweet ceremony. The next thing they knew, Reverend Thompson was giving instructions for Andre to salute his bride. Andre and Yolanda kissed for an eternity, knowing that everything they were now doing was blessed by God.

After the ceremony everyone sat down to a delightful dinner. Yolanda could hardly believe her eyes as each course was presented. Everything just kept getting better and better. The hors d'oevers consisted of spinach and smoked Gouda poppers, crab stuffed mushrooms, and shrimp cocktails. The entrée came next, and the wedding party feasted on Chicken Marsala with wine and mushroom sauce, nutted wild rice, and carrots Marsala. Finally, dessert was served and everyone raved over the lemon curd tarts and the pecan bourbon pie.

Yolanda and Andre cut the small wedding cake. It was a red velvet cake with butter cream icing and was decorated with ivory calla lilies. They fed each other and posed for what seemed like the millionth photograph of the day. Andre and Yolanda looked at each other and knew that it was time to go. They both were ready to give themselves to one another.

Yolanda and Andre settled into the limousine for the ride to Chateau Élan Inn. Andre had reserved a suite and could not wait to get there to make love to his bride.

CHAPTER 31

Yolanda and Andre arrived at their suite and shared a long passionate kiss and looked deep into each other's eyes for what seemed like an eternity. Andre carried Yolanda across the threshold and into their room. They held each other so tightly, that it was hard for either of them to breathe.

"I have something that I would like to share with you, Yolanda." Andre reached into his tux pocket and retrieved an envelope. He began to read to Yolanda from the beautiful stationary that was inside excerpts from the Song of Solomon. Yolanda cried as Andre relayed through scripture how he was smitten with her and desired her. Yolanda thought that it was the most beautiful thing on earth.

Song of Solomon 4
1Behold, thou art fair, my love; behold, thou art fair; thou hast doves' eyes within thy locks: thy hair is as a flock of goats, that appear from mount Gilead.

2Thy teeth are like a flock of sheep that are even shorn, which came up from the washing; whereof every one bear twins, and none is barren among them.

3Thy lips are like a thread of scarlet, and thy speech is comely: thy temples are like a piece of a pomegranate within thy locks.

4Thy neck is like the tower of David builded for an armoury, whereon there hang a thousand bucklers, all shields of mighty men.

5Thy two breasts are like two young roes that are twins, which feed among the lilies.

6Until the day break, and the shadows flee away, I will get me to the mountain of myrrh, and to the hill of frankincense.

7Thou art all fair, my love; there is no spot in thee.

8Come with me from Lebanon, my spouse, with me from Lebanon: look from the top of Amana, from the top of Shenir and Hermon, from the lions' dens, from the mountains of the leopards.

9Thou hast ravished my heart, my sister, my spouse; thou hast ravished my heart with one of thine eyes, with one chain of thy neck.

10How fair is thy love, my sister, my spouse! how much better is thy love than wine! and the smell of thine ointments than all spices!

11Thy lips, O my spouse, drop as the honeycomb: honey and milk are under thy tongue; and the smell of thy garments is like the smell of Lebanon.

12A garden inclosed is my sister, my spouse; a spring shut up, a fountain sealed.

13Thy plants are an orchard of pomegranates, with pleasant fruits; camphire, with spikenard,

14Spikenard and saffron; calamus and cinnamon, with all trees of frankincense; myrrh and aloes, with all the chief spices:

15A fountain of gardens, a well of living waters, and streams from Lebanon.

16Awake, O north wind; and come, thou south; blow upon my garden, that the spices thereof may flow out. Let my beloved come into his garden, and eat his pleasant fruits.

Andre placed the stationary on the bed and kissed Yolanda again.

"You will never ever know how happy I am this day. I vow to be the best husband that I can possibly be, only with help from the Lord. Now, why don't we freshen up so that we can do what we have longed to do forever." Andre playfully patted Yolanda's rear as she walked towards the bathroom.

After taking a nice relaxing bath together, Yolanda shooed Andre out of the bathroom so that she could slide into her lingerie. Yolanda had kept the lingerie that she had chosen for her first escapade with Andre, but had never worn it. As she slid into the mocha silk gown with plunging necklines and matching silk heels, Yolanda knew that this time, everything was right, and God was pleased.

Andre sat up in bed as Yolanda entered the room. Her countenance was beautiful, and he could not wait to make love to her. Andre got out of bed and picked Yolanda up, cradling her in his arms and gave her small kisses on her lips. He lay her down gently on the bed and kissed what seemed to Yolanda like every hair on her head. He then began to work his way downward to her eyelids, nose mouth and ears. Yolanda felt her temperature rise another degree with every kiss and felt she would explode. Andre licked and kissed her neck, tracing imaginary circles with his tongue. He then spent what seemed like hours kissing and softly caressing her breasts. He made his way down to the wine goblet that was her navel, and made Yolanda mad with want as he traced slow circles with his tongue. Her inner and outer thighs relished in the attention that he gave. The back of her knees thanked him for every sensual kiss that he planted there. Her ankles and toes blessed him for the detail and kindness that he left there. He and Yolanda both gasped as they become one. Yolanda felt waves of passion flood her and allowed herself to be free and receive the pleasure that Andre was giving her. Andre and Yolanda played in rhythm a song that only they knew, and neither of them was in a rush to complete. Afterward, as their bodies glistened with sweat, Andre and Yolanda cuddled and kissed more, and sleep came easy and peacefully.

CHAPTER 32

Andre watched with excitement as Yolanda approached the podium to preach her initial sermon. It had been three years since they'd gotten married and moved to Atlanta. They both had been counseled by Reverend Thompson after they moved, and he had gladly spent those years imparting the Word, and helping them both to become whole. He recognized that God was telling him that it was time to pass the torch. Reverend Thompson took some flack from a few of the parishioners who had heard about Yolanda and Andre's affair and did not want them to join the church. But, Reverend Thompson would not budge and asked that anyone who was without sin to cast the first stone. No one moved, and the issue was dead.

Yolanda had done a lot of soul-searching and knew exactly who she was and what she wanted out of life. She could now tell you how much money she had in the bank down to the penny. Her long, permed black hair was now a cacophony of natural twists highlighted with cinnamon streaks. She was enrolled in school to complete her Doctorate in Psychology. Yolanda had also started a non-profit group called A Better Way, which provided survivors of domestic violence emergency shelter. The group also offered batterers a six week class to give alternatives to abusing their spouse. She figured that if she could help one person not live the nightmare that she had, it would all be worth it. Yolanda also led the marriage ministry at church, and found great pleasure in teaching. The women at church seemed to welcome her with open arms, and Yolanda finally felt comfortable. She was also no longer afraid to say what she wants in bed or if she was or was not satisfied. She knew how to be a submissive wife, which means she respected her husband. It was easy to submit to Andre, because he treated her like a queen, and loved her as Jesus loved the church. Yolanda finally understood what peace and happiness was, and most important of all, how to obtain it.

Donovan pointed excitedly to his mother and yells "mommy" as Yolanda began to take her text. Andre laughed and whispered in Donovan's ear to quiet down.

Yolanda began to speak. "Before I get to my text, and give the Word that God has given me, there are a couple of things that I would like to say. I know some of you all know me and some of you grew up with me, driving all the way down to Atlanta to support me. Some of you may also know about my past, and you don't even think I should be up here preaching today. But, I know the Bible says that God has not called us to uncleanness, but unto holiness. He goes on to tell us to "Be ye holy for I am Holy". In the book of Romans the eighth Chapter and the thirtieth and thirty first verse says "Moreover whom he did predestinate, them he also called: and whom he called he also justified: and whom he justified, them he also glorified. What shall we then say to these things? If God be for us, who can be against us?" Yolanda paused as the congregation belted out Amen's and Hallelujah's in concordance with the beat of the organ.

"So, don't get so hung up on my past that you will not be able to see what God wants to do in your future."

After another five minute praise break filled with dancing and shouting, Yolanda continued.

"I would also like to thank my mentor and friend, Reverend Thompson for imparting his God-given anointing in me. God has truly blessed me by allowing him to be a part of my life.

And last, but certainly not least, I want to thank my husband for standing by me. He is my best friend and the father of my child, and I will spend the rest of my life gladly loving him."

"Now, let's get down to business and get the Word of the day from Our Father." Yolanda prayed a short sincere prayer. "Everyone open your Bibles to Job the twenty third Chapter, verses eight, nine, and ten." Yolanda began to read and she could almost feel the power of the Holy Ghost falling down. She continued to read.

"But if I go to the east, he is not there; if I go to the west, I do not find him. When he is at work in the north; I do not see him; But he knows the way that I take; when he has tested me; I will come forth as gold." Yolanda began to relay to the congregation how she felt when Timothy died and everyone called her everything but a child of God.

"I wanted to turn my back on God because I felt like I had been mistreated when my abusive husband was alive, and I was treated worse after he died. I felt that if that was what I would continue to experience trying to live for Him; then I didn't want to be Christian anymore. I was depressed and I wanted to die. But, He didn't give up on me, even though I had given up on Him." Yolanda then proceeded to break the word down to the congregation. After teaching, Yolanda beckoned those that were lost to come to Christ, saying today was the day of salvation. Hordes of people, young and old flocked to the altar, crying and wailing, some rejoicing.

Yolanda could not hold back the tears that streamed down her face. She felt as if she finally knew her purpose in life. She had walked into her calling; to reconcile the lost to Christ, to be a wife and mother, then to be the Pastor of Philadelphia Baptist Church. No other order would do. Yolanda had learned from Timothy's mistakes that the divine order was God, Family, and then the Church- not God, the Church, and then Family. She let the congregation know up front that she would not compromise her beliefs, and they accepted her terms. After a rousing sermon and productive altar call, everyone hugged Yolanda and Andre after church, welcoming them.

Yolanda, Andre and Donovan sat on the porch swing and relaxed. Andre and Yolanda both felt like a weight had been lifted. Yolanda never thought she would become a preacher, but thanked God every day that He chose her to carry his Word. Yolanda and Andre cuddled and kissed, and laughed as Donovan tried to stop them.

"No, daddee, my mommy!" Donovan climbed into Yolanda's lap and planted a sloppy wet kiss on her lips. Andre and Yolanda chuckled and Yolanda squeezed Donovan tightly. Yolanda still thanked God every day for blessing her with a child. She recognized that her child would live and not die. Yolanda sat and reflected over her life, and could not remember a time when she was as happy as she was now. She finally was at peace, and gave all of the glory to God.

After putting Donovan to bed, Yolanda and Andre rushed to get into bed themselves. After much fasting and prayer in preparation for her initial sermon, they both were ready to come together as one again. Andre and Yolanda made love to each other for what seemed like hours, absolutely sure of their love and commitment to one another. Andre and Yolanda spooned and Andre softly kissed the back of Yolanda's neck.

"Many waters cannot quench love" Andre spoke as he continued to run his tongue along Yolanda's neck.

"Neither can the floods drown it," Yolanda offered, pressing herself back into Andre's arms as far as physically possible.

"Nothing can come in between what we share."

"Nothing and no one", Yolanda stated as she drifted off to sleep, confident in the last words that she had spoken.

About the Author

The lure of enticing words has always captivated Pamela D. Rice. Even at the tender age of two, this soulful native South Carolinian would intensely gaze at books, pretending to read and embrace the content within the pages. Pamela became an avid reader, and soon found a natural progression and flair for expressing herself through illuminating words which resulted in her becoming a published poet while in the eighth grade.

Known for her stimulating and thought-provoking views, Pamela possesses a fervor for creatively giving a voice to victims who suffer in silence, afraid to speak for themselves. Inspired by everyday situations and social exchanges, Pamela has always enjoyed observing people and dissecting their interactions; this hobby became her muse. It is her desire to become a literary vessel that brings light to the social ill of domestic violence and its reach beyond all racial, cultural and socio-economic class. Through inspirational prose, she is destined to heal the human soul.

When Pamela is not writing, she enjoys spending time with her family, traveling, and exploring other cultures.

Learn more at www.PamelaDRice.com.

Peace In The Storm Publishing, LLC is the winner of the
2009 African American Literary Award for
Independent Publisher of the Year.

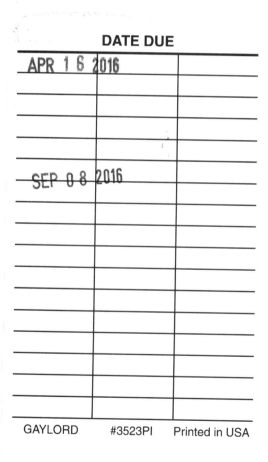

DATE DUE

APR 1 6 2016		
SEP 0 8 2016		

GAYLORD   #3523PI   Printed in USA